THE BLACK TRITON

H. M. Sanders

Acknowledgements

This book would not have come into being without the assistance and help given to me by my editor, Karen Fisher. Her good humor, kindness, and intelligence once again have saved my bacon. I would also like to thank Kim and Jeff Nichols, who allowed me to write much of this book in their lovely old island home, during the 2020 covid pandemic. I thank them both for their generous gifts in a strange and dangerous time.

Once again, I acknowledge my partner, Sara Bayer, for her compassionate patience and tolerance of the creative process.

For the Blue House

CHAPTER ONE

The Color of Water

The first memory Fela had was of her mother's hands carefully working colors into shapes on parchment; stick figures and patterns...a yellow arrow streaking across blue sky, a man on a brown horse, a red bird winging towards a triangle of mountains in sable black, new grass green.

As she grew older, her mother's paintings began to take on meaning. Fela knew her mother painted them to help people with sickness, with healing. She saw the flying arrow chasing a spirit, the red bird taking a message to a dead ancestor. Soon she was helping her mother roll out the parchments and flatten them with stones; she brought her mother the bowls of resin, pigments, and water. At night, in front of the fire, her father fashioned horsehair brushes. Sometimes her mother let her handle them.

The best times were when her uncle visited from across

the mountains. For her mother, he brought spices that smelled like raisins and honeysuckle. Once, for Fela, he brought a flute made from deer bone, ornamented with brass. He showed her how to play it. Then he brought an ivory carving of a strange animal, a seal it was called, on a leather pendant. The seal came from the sea, he said, like his own family. Her uncle's hands were gentle, softer than her father's, and as he spoke of the sea it was as if he spoke of something sacred, something fabulous. Her mother said she was too young to wear such a thing, and her father had taken it for safekeeping.

Best of all, Fela loved the rowdy nights after Father and Uncle Pib had drinks from the brown bottle. Then Uncle Pib retrieved his pipes and her father got out his drums. They would play until very late. Her mother enjoyed some of this, but always went to bed early, taking Fela with her. Fela would wait until her mother slept, then sneak back out and dance wildly in front of the fire to the lilting sound of the pipes until she fell asleep in her father's lap.

As she grew older, her mother taught her the plants and rocks that made the healing colors, and, her mother whispered: all colors were good, but blue was the queen, the palinisar of them all; the blue magic came from a precious rock she could only find deep in the forest and Fela's agile mind took this and tumbled with it.

Between the strange sea animal called a seal her uncle had shown her, and the secrecy behind it, and the sea stories Fela had heard or imagined, the color blue became linked in her mind to the sea. When her mother worked with blue...cerulean blue, aquamarine blue, midnight blue...imaginary waves lapped at Fela's feet, and the strange dark eyes of the seal watched her. She imagined the bright shining blue water kissing her toes the way it did when she went to the creek to fetch water for the goats, and in the patterns her mother painted she saw a great reverberating blue sheet of water that stretched, calm and beneficent, to the ends of the earth, so far that it touched the rocky talons of dragon-land, and made her thrill deep inside with the alien feel of it. When she interrogated her father, he said the sea was like a thousand creeks all worked into one, with sand and rocks along its shores, mighty with hidden power that killed the ignorant, and drowned the unschooled by filling their lungs with salt water. Fela saw the sea in the blue of the sky, in the polished gems of her mother's worked silver bracelet, even in the eyes of her baby brother Ben. When her father said pirates roamed and hidden islands remained secret, she felt a tug beneath her breastbone that wound into her belly and made her eyes long for the sight of it. It frightened her. It called to her. In bed, she lay and imagined: storm-tossed water concealing the heaving fins and coracle-shaped eyes of monsters. In fitful dreams, black bodies of water swallowed the view of land, spume flew from waves so huge her fear made her struggle to draw breath. On the other side she knew was her family's home and everything familiar, the orchards and rolling green hills, the farms and goat pens and the courtyard where she played...and that they were all lost to her and she floundered, taking on water that made her heavy, paralyzed. Those were bad dreams, and there were better dreams of the sea, but this one she had had many times. She had told no one about them. It was childish. Her mother said she imagined too much.

When her mother went to the forest for blue stones, she always went by herself. Fela wanted to go. When her mother came home, Fela was full of questions. "How old are the woods?" she asked.

"Very old."

"Does Ocan live there?"

Her mother smiled. Ocan was the protector of the hearth and all who lived at the hearth. "He might. But probably not. Ocan lives in the ashes of the grating, nutkin. That's why we light candles in the hearth on certain days. To honor him. There are other spirits in the woods."

"Please, take me with you."

"No," her mother said. "You're still too small."

"I'm not small!" she said.

"You're only ten. The woods are dangerous."

"Why are the woods dangerous?"

"Tonkirs," her father said.

What kind of tonkirs? she wondered. Were they poisonous? Did they bite? If they were dangerous, then didn't her mother need protection and help? Fela ran over to her father's armor where it stood on its wooden rack. Then, respectfully, but quickly, she pulled down the helmet and donned it, despite her father's doleful clucking. She marched back to her parents beside the hearth, puffed out her chest and said, "I will protect you, mother. I will!" Her father only laughed, he laughed until tears streamed down his eyes like they did when Uncle Pib came to visit and they drank what her mother called the brew from hell.

She knew her father's tears weren't a good sign. Even her mother had begun laughing.

"When will I be old enough?" she asked.

"Next year," her father said. "When you're eleven."

From that time, she began counting. She was ten, then she would be eleven. At thirteen, she would be a woman! The time, her mother said, when young men brought flowers, and pots of honey for the family, and worked on the farm to show their dedication and their ability to woo her. She didn't know what wooing was, but it was how her mother and father had met, though they hadn't married until later. Her mother said she could be married by thirteen, it was true, but best to wait until she was sixteen or so.

For a year, she waited, ready for the time when she could go with her mother. She skipped and sang and sucked the sweet nectar from the honeysuckle that grew on the compound wall. She helped her father. She helped her mother. She kept her grandfather company. He liked to doze in the sun in the morning. He smelled rank, like old horse blankets, and rarely knew where he was or who she was, but on his better days, he smiled while she sang, and gave her small candies. She played with her baby brother, Ben. He was a thoughtful baby, quite content. When Fela began her shouts of poetic joy, he launched into wordless songs, singing along with her. She called it singing, but her father called it the shriek of the magpie.

She gathered and hoarded secret and ancient things to put into her magic box. Her father carved her a small figure of Kel, the god of war. She put Kel into the box. She had the stub of a candle, an offering for Kel. She had broken bits of charcoal, for drawing. She had precious stones. One was small and round like a palinisar's jewel.

Her mother brought back soft fragile rock from the creekbed. Fela watched, mesmerized, as her mother ground stone on stone, rhythmically, palms down, shoulders moving, the sound hard on the ears. She saw the sweat gather on her mother's forehead, saw the miraculous powdered yellow her mother's efforts birthed, the yellow of buttercups, or juicy summer plums, or aged cheese her father hoarded. Her mother rolled the pigment with sticky resin, then gave a bit to her, the sun's light captured from clay, a talisman, an example of her mother's wondrous skill. This, she also put into her box.

Finally, the day arrived. Afelanua had been named in the old language after the apple trees, for she had been born in late summer, as the golden apples were ripening on the boughs. And now the apples were ripening again, and she would go with her mother into the forest.

That morning she woke, ecstatic, in a fantastic land of blue pearls and mysterious forests. "I know where the best blue is, sky blue, egg-blue, sea-blue, the sea, the sea, the sea…." Fela began her morning dance around the great room. "Mama. I'm ready to go. I've got my box."

Umila shifted Ben on her hip as she stirred the barley porridge. Ben gabbled and clung.

"Mama mama mama, when shall we go? Shall I go get Papa? Shall I get your basket? Shall I…"

"You shall get us bowls. And please calm down! Please."

Fela slumped, crestfallen. Her mother softened. "Just a little, pumpkin-cake. Your mother needs to think."

"Yes mama. Bowls! Bowls bowls bowls…." Fela dashed to set the table, fantasizing about the forest, the black marauders and the ruby tonkirs, old magic and blue stones, and warriors on horses attacking them both while she, the courageous, the righteous, protected them all. Then her mother could grind her colors in peace, and Ben would worship her, his elder sister and his sovereign ruler, and all would be perfect.

They ate. Her father came in from saddling the horses, and said he would mind Ben.

Finally, they were ready. They mounted their horses,

and set away on the road toward Dunning Province.

At the township's gates, they turned east, into the forest.

"How far is it?" she asked.

"It's several hours ride," her mother answered. "You'll have to be patient, and quiet. Can you do it?"

"Yes." She looked around, thoughtfully.

"Soon we'll get to the dark pool, and I'll need to stop there for a while. We can eat our cheese and fruit then."

Fela nodded.

They rode down the shadowy path in companionable silence. The birds cried and sang, and sang again, all around them in the leafy woods, and clumps of buckthorn gleamed red in the mid-day sun.

At last, they came to a wide place in the trail, and here was the pool of which her mother had spoken, its water as still as a dark sheet of metal.

Her mother dismounted. She was wearing a long muslin skirt, light, for the warmer weather. Fela got off her horse, Apple.

"Why have we stopped here, Mama?"

"Well. The earth is our mother. The sun is our father. Yes?"

"Yes. So…?"

"One of earth's children is water. Water comes up from the earth's center, from the very womb of mother earth herself. And so…" Umila's voice faded as she rummaged in her packs.

"So?"

Her mother took from her bag clippings of rosemary and bay, and twined them together. "…So artisans…like me… give thanks to the earth's bounty. Water is the course by which magic gets half its power. The sun gives the other half of magic's power…and when the two combine…poof! You get an invisible fog that wraps the world." Her mother smiled.

"So…we give an offering to the water spirits? For Magic?"

"Well, creativity is a kind of magic, nurtured by mother earth and provoked by father fire. Since water is one of the ways earth nurtures magic and creativity, and since I'm attuned to water, the way you are attuned to wood…"

"…and Papa to wood…"

"Yes, you are like your father that way…oak-skinned and hard-headed…" Her mother laughed at her, and Fela grinned.

"So that's why we're here? To thank the water spirits?"

"Yes. Now, wait here. This won't take long, Mousekin."

Quickly, her mother disappeared. The horses grazed. For a while, Fela waited and watched. She had brought her box, but here, in the forest, the objects in it seemed less wonderful and mysterious. Whereas the more she looked into the forest, the more mysterious it seemed.

The banks sloped steeply toward the pool. Shady rocks and trees were edged with tiny fingers of yellow-green moss that grew in abundance over all damp things. The fiddlehead ferns had unraveled. Moss dipped into the water. The shore was lined with smooth round stones, as old as mountains and earth. A decaying log with shredded edges lay in the water, like a bridge that went nowhere.

A deer trail went in the other direction, into the forest, and she rose and followed it, always checking back over her shoulder, to make sure she knew where her mother was. The trail led into an old and open stand of cedars. The ground beneath them was clear and softly carpeted with old needles.

Very little could grow beneath big cedars. They were powerful trees, with powerful spirits, and Fela was respectful amongst them. Beyond the clearing was a cascade of old tumbled boulders, the size of corn cribs and bigger. Fela went to see, to look for special stones. She knew that anything she found here would hold the cedar's secrets. If she found a small stone, she could take it home, and in her bed at night she could listen to it, and remember this day and hear the cedars' branches still creaking above her, protecting her mother and her.

She put her hand on a big smooth boulder and time suddenly dropped away.

She stood still in front of a formless place. The only thing she could still feel was the boulder, cold under her palm.

Then she saw a man. On his knees. The man was sobbing, gurgling. Spittle ran thick down his chin and his long black moustaches were wet with his own tears and blood. She saw, or felt - she couldn't be sure - his black helmet rolled off to the side. She saw the fissure across its crown. She clearly felt him, was in him, or around him...he was loaded with despair. She felt the sorrow and saw his wife, his two young sons, his baby girl...she could feel it all, she could feel his life draining away. And she could hear his voice and could not recognize the words but she knew what he was saying.

"I've never begged for anything! I'm begging now..."

"Get up, Tundin slag-heap. Get up and face your death."

Fela could hear another voice but it was distant. In horrible clarity, she only knew him. The one who begged. The one who loved his wife with an emotion she had no words for, but it was bitter and needy, awful in its alien darkness and spread. The words came out of her, or him, she couldn't tell.

"I'm begging you. I have a family. They're my life…"

The other voice laughed as from a cloud, obscured. "That's over now. Pray, or close your eyes, leave off your begging. Face your death like a warrior."

Fela convulsed as the man took the strike. There was a white-hot desperate search to say goodbye, goodbye to a faceless woman holding a bundle in her arms and then… emptiness. Like…blank clay. Mud. Shapeless. Formless. Like the round, cold stone beneath her fingers. She slipped away and even the cold of the stone under her hand faded.

When it happened, when she heard the child scream, Umila knew it was a tonkir. Hard, cold anger turned her into her own armored monster as she gripped her small hammer and pick, launched herself off the ground, and pounded through the salal and thorny wild roses for her precious, her one downy-cheeked girl-child. A black marauder, if she could catch the animal and kill it, things would be all right, all right…a ruby tonkir was not as dangerous but this wasn't ruby territory…she ran and ran and thrashed. Wild raspberries tore red welts on her uncaring skin. She followed a deer trail through aspen, into a cedar grove, beyond to a rockfall, and there was her child. Umila's heart pounded. Her breath was dry fire in her throat. The lump of her child's body was still, face down on the needle-covered floor. Soft lichen-covered mounds of boulders, huge and shapeless as giant potatoes, loomed everywhere, a kind of mute stone garden.

Umila looked around…over all the rocks, the trees, up in the boughs…her arms and legs would not stop shaking. But no animal, no sign of animal, no low guarding hiss of a tonkir, no sign of a provoked deer, no big cat, or wild wolf. "Fela? Fela?"

The child did not move. She was still. Her bobbed black hair shrouded her skull and she was face down in the cedar needles. Umila hurried to her daughter. She cradled her in her arms and pushed the child's hair out of her face. Breathing. No marks. Her hands moved over the summer shift, felt the acorn-brown skin at the chest, checked the arms, moved her little necklace with the seal that her Uncle Pib had brought for her, but nothing. No blood. But breath in her baby child. Umila held Fela to her breast and cradled the child and prayed her name. "Fela. Baby girl. Mousekin. Come back. Wake up. Wake up."

She rocked the child in her arms and her mind rolled through what might have happened. Had she eaten a poisonous plant? But there were no plants here, among the cedars... Not attacked, was it a seizure? Some children began to have seizures as they neared womanhood...but there was no frothing, no eye-rolling. The child didn't shake or tremble. She was simply unconscious.

Umila was rampaging through her mind for a possible clue, something she'd missed, when Fela's eyes fluttered open. "Mama?"

"Mouse. Mousekin."

Fela hadn't been held like this since she was a baby. She squirmed. But her head hurt, and then she remembered what had happened. "Where is he?" She whispered.

Umila was crying, and furious at the same time. "Mouselet, did you eat something? Did you hit your head? I've told you to be careful, child, Fela, you must be careful, it's too easy to die..."

"But I didn't do anything. There was a man."

Umila stilled, clutching Fela. Fela left off her squirming. "What man? Where?"

"I don't know. He was here. I touched one of the rocks, and he died. He was begging for his life. His helmet was on the ground over there, like father's but...it was different. It had etchings on it. It had an odd shape."

Umila didn't move, but stared at Fela. "There's no one here. There's no helmet. How do you feel?"

She blinked her eyes, blue, like her father's, innocent, cloudy now though, with the memory of what had happened. "My head hurts. Tired. That's all. Is he here? He had blood in his moustaches." She twisted, trying to look around.

Umila remained motionless with the child in her arms, and the thought, the idea slunk into her mind sideways. She might be one of them. She could be. She was eleven, and that's when it started. She closed her eyes and fear welled. Not this. Not this. She wanted a normal life for her child, a laughing young man to take her to dances, children and weaving and a household of warmth and worship. Not this. Not dark visions from obscurity, the domain of witches' webs and the black pits of terror, spinning in a smoke-filled corner and summoning demons. To be hunted by her fellow villagers and called a monster.

"We're going home."

"But we have to find him..."

"You're hurt. We're going home. Get your things."

Fela lay in her warm downy bed and listened to her parent's voices carry. The sound rose and fell like the wind that buffeted the home sometimes during storms.

"Are you sure it was a vision? She didn't hit her head, or

eat something, she wasn't attacked?"

"I'm not blind! There's no marks on her…"

"You don't have to yell, love."

"You try finding your only daughter lying on the ground like death and see what it does to you! I shouldn't have taken her…"

"There's nothing wrong with what you did. We both decided. She's old enough."

There was a pause. Fela turned so that her head was propped up off of her pillow. She wanted to hear everything. It made her feel afraid, what her parents were saying. But she didn't know why.

"If she is, Umila, we have to face it."

"There could be another reason. It might just be…a solitary thing. It might never happen again."

"Umila. Come here."

"Leave off."

"Just come sit beside me, by the fire. Please."

Silence for minutes. Fela waited, breathless.

Her mother, sobbing. She couldn't make it all out. "I don't want her to be an outcast. I don't want her to be homeless. She's my only daughter, my baby."

"My sweet, black rose. She'll never be homeless. She'll never be an outcast. Nameless, perhaps. Enduil. But not homeless."

"Witches!" her mother's hissing voice. "Summoning dark monsters! Coiling evil hexes around good people! Burning babies to death! I've heard the stories!"

"Umila. For Tun's sake. That's the worst kind of gossip…"

"But that's what she'll hear! That's what she'll be called!"

"Umila. You're not making any sense. Pib…"

"Oh yes Pib now there's a fine shining example. Sitting around with his dusty books, putting off his marriage for years…"

"Stop it. He's my best friend. And it's she who's put the thing off. Why are you so bitter about him?"

Silence. She loved her Uncle. Why was mother so angry?

"Because it's dangerous. What he's doing. What you two are doing, with those scrolls. It's so dangerous. And now, this…there's got to be something we can do…" Her mother's voice sounded wild in a way that made Fela's skin prick tight.

"I could find her a teacher. There are still people out east, I've heard, who know the old high magic. Not that dark stuff of wet feathers and dead lambs. And…Pib…"

"I didn't mean to insult your friend. I'm just worried."

"I know."

More silence. Fela strained her ears listening.

"He's one, you know. From his pa's side."

Her mother's voice, very low. "What?"

"Ayah. I never told you because it never came up. His father had some strange sea magic in his blood."

"How could you not tell me?"

"For the fear I'm getting now. I've not known a kinder, more generous man than Pib…"

More silence. Fela was shocked as well by this information. "Strange sea magic." The words slid around in her mind like wild, jeweled serpents. What did it mean?

"You're right. I just…need some time to think about this. All right? I want to teach her to bake cakes, Alivar. Not control her visions!"

"Aren't your paintings, my love, a kind of vision?"

Dead silence. She thought she heard cloth shifting.

"It's different." But there was a strange tone to her mother's voice. Then only silence, and the snapping of the fire in the hearth, and whispers, and finally the candle went out and she heard them go to bed.

Fela tucked back under her covers and pulled her knees up to her chest. Her Uncle Pib might be one, one of the people of which her mother was scared. She closed her eyes, and from her memory she looked at the strange thing that had happened that day in her mind the way a thief might admire a hard-won purse under night's secret cover.

She remembered admiring the tiny red flowers near a clump of deer moss at the base of one of the powerful rocks in the grove. She had put her left hand out to steady herself. Her hand...had it felt warm? She thought hard. It had been... perhaps not warmth, but a glue-like connection, an odd thick feeling, almost like an enormous spider web's stickiness that ran from her palm and through her entire body. But when it had reached her mind a red, vibrant image had filled her inner seeing. The man had been so real...she had felt everything, seen everything, images from his life had blasted through her and now in the quiet of the warm home, she sifted through them, but it felt as if she had opened doors on some private thing, and she backed out of the memories. The man had been loved by many warriors; they were blurred behind him and around him; she felt their support in his courage. He had had a family...she could feel the protective surge for the children, and some darker, fierce feeling for the woman that frightened her. Fela closed her eyes and shut the door on the memory. It was still so powerful...if she looked closely it was still as if it had just happened, but at least she couldn't feel the scream of his death any longer in her mind, or the wild searching that happened afterwards. That had left her feeling as if someone had drained her own soul out along with the man's, as he died.

Fela rolled over towards the window. The memory of the man felt like an especially strong dream, a dream that was beginning to unravel. She looked at her hand in the stone-white glow of the moon, and wondered. She turned her head and watched the dark fields of her family's land, and soon sleep took her into its soft cocoon.

CHAPTER TWO

Arguments and Magic

He and Umila fought. They made love that night. He tried to apologize to her with his body, but her distance persisted.

She moved around her dairy and counter where the bread rose, banging bowls as Alivar reasoned with her again, softly, persistently. Why hide a gift? The Enduil brought peace and rituals with their magic and the worship of Tun.

She would not reply. Her soft face became subtly rigid. The melting quality of her eyes, usually so dark and languid, became edged with anger.

Finally the children began to get cross. Fela dropped a crockery and burst into tears, and Ben wailed in sympathy.

Alivar rode out with his pipe and stayed away for half the day.

His daughter's simple worry tore at him. There was so

much she didn't know. His mind swerved from the horror stories: of Nameless whose bodies had never been found. Why shouldn't he let her mother hide her for as long as possible?

But no. The truth was paramount. The facts of the world, Pib's secret, the tonkirs' ways--if he didn't teach her, who would? Who would give her both truths, not just the light?

He returned, and, after the children were asleep, he tried again.

"Let me take her. I'll find her a teacher."

Umila slammed both palms onto the counter, her lips tightened in a fierce rictus. "I don't want her hounded! I want her married and happy! I want protection for her! I don't want her always wondering what other people might think, what other people might do, to her, or behind her back! Curses whispered to her, her children sneered at...."

"It's because of your father, isn't it?" Alivar whispered.

Umila whipped around to him and her face looked like one who had taken poison. "Don't you bring him into this!"

"He couldn't help what he was..."

"He ruined my mother's life!"

"He died because he didn't know his own power! If he had known..." Alivar moved towards her, pleading.

But Umila turned her back on him and her voice pulsed with bright fury. "Stop it! I know what you're trying to do! Stop it!" She overturned the crockery onto the floured board with too much force and baby Ben began to wail in the other room.

Alivar was furious at his wife's blindness. His chest went cold, and he could feel the tendrils of ice invade the edges of his own eyes. "I'm taking her. I'll not have a child of mine helpless and ignorant in the face of something she was meant to have."

He left the kitchen with no more words.

Fela knew that papa and Uncle Pib had made countless forays deep to the east of the Tundin Valley, into the badlands, but this was her first trip in that direction.

"Papa."

"Yes?" Her father tamped the tobacco into the bowl. He leaned over, his mouth still too closed, and lit a twig on fire. They both watched the end of the twig go to a red glow.

"Where are we going?"

"Mouse. We're going deep into the east to find a teacher for you. There are more people, like you, with rare gifts who might be able to help you."

She took up the wood poker and jabbed at one of the larger pieces of wood in the fire. "Mama didn't want us to go, did she?"

"No. She didn't."

"Why is it bad to be Nameless?" Fela hugged her knees to herself.

Her father lowered his pipe. "Where did you get that notion?"

"I heard you and mama talking. The night after I saw the man get killed in the cedar forest."

"Ah. Fela. Your mama is frightened for you. Neither of us know much about your gift. Whether it's a danger to you, or others, or…what it means." His mouth tightened, watching her. "We don't want you to get hurt. It's why I want to find a teacher for you. When you have children of your own, you'll understand. You're my most precious thing. And you are your mama's most precious thing." He turned his pipe in his hands. Fela listened intently. She rarely had her father all to herself. "And it's a painful thing, because we know…you're not ours. You belong to yourself." He smiled at her.

"I'm yours, papa." Her nose wrinkled.

"Yeah, but not for long, pumpkin. A nice young man will take you. You'll have babies of your own. You'll have adventures of your own."

She nodded. She thought. "Uncle Pib…is he Nameless? And what is secret sea magic?"

Her father smiled. He leaned back. "Pib's got the gift of sincerity. And music. And…" He closed his eyes, and thought for a moment. Then he leaned in close to her, his eyes gleaming in the firelight, "and…he's got a hidden magic to him, the kind that sea serpents guarding treasure chests full of gold shields, and pearl amulets have in abundance! Remember the tale of Old Nerea, the serpent beneath the sea, who stole the jewel from the crab-people?"

Fela's eyes brightened. "Yes!" She squealed a little. "Tell it again!"

Her father closed his eyes and stretched theatrically. "Oh, you don't want to hear that old story."

"Yes! Yes I do! Oh please please please…" She completely forgot she was eleven years old. She squealed and clapped her hands.

Her father put down his pipe. "Well, all right then. But just this once." He stood up slowly and threw his robes from his sides in a great air of princely boredom. Then he stalked to the other side of the fire and spread his cloak about him, like great wide wings. Fela gasped.

"Oh, then, once when the world was young and volcanoes steamed and dragons rode the bright, hot air, the ocean teemed with all manner of creatures." He paused. "They're all gone now." He narrowed his eyes, for he knew his daughter's obsession with the ocean. "But then...back then, when there were dragons with iron scales, and eels the size of islands, and great blind lizards that sunned themselves in the moonlight...one such creature, hidden in the deep, was the old sea-serpentess Nerea. Oh, she was a mean sea-monster. She teased sailors' ships and tossed them on her back! Like this!" Alivar threw sand into the air and Fela jumped. "She ate huge whales for breakfast and burped up their bones!" He feigned vomiting into the fire, holding his belly. Fela hiccoughed with laughter. "But when she stole the old crab-king's jewel, well." Alivar's eyes narrowed. "The crab-people didn't take too kindly to that. Do you know what they did?"

Fela's eyes grew round. "No! What! What did they do?"

Alivar spread both hands out in front of them. "They held a giant counsel, and the greatest of all the crab mages, they called him Corazul...he had great blue claws covered with barnacles...."

"What's a..."

Alivar hissed at her. "Wait! Listen! He had great blue claws, covered with barnacles, and great beady eyes on stalks that waved above his head, and a beautiful seal-bone inlaid with sea emeralds for doing magic with! And do you know what he did?"

"No! No! What happened!" Fela stared, entranced.

"The great crab counsel decided to curse Nerea for stealing their precious jewel! They cursed her so that she could not come onto dry land, and visit her husband the Wind! And to this day, great storms toss the ocean, and rip the trees from islands, and it's Nerea, enraged and roaring, whipping up the ocean with her great scaly tail, trying to get to her husband, the Wind!" Alivar stood up, and straightened his cloak.

"Please! Another!"

"It's bed time for you." He stood wrapped in his cloak and frowning at the moon. Fela thought him very handsome and full of important thoughts.

"Please, just one more...I promise I won't ask any questions."

"Hmm. Well. One more."

He flourished his cloak, and then sat down very slowly, with a great deal of frowning and exaggerated movements. He stirred the fire so that sparks went flying up in a curtain of flashing red. "I will tell you the story of How the Otter Stole the Moons." He opened his arms wide.

"Hold!

Wait!

Listen: it is coming.

The children who danced on the earth

long long ago

This is the time that sister otter

stole the moons from brother tonkir.

Once, in the spring of our time

before humans or dragons made their way

in the dust, and tonkir children flourished like sand on a beach,

tonkir was coming back from the red world

his cheeks full of good things to eat.

Now he was happy. Now he was fat

and his belly full.

He thought: I have much food, and I am tired, and the sun is warm.

I can rest a little and be home soon.

He curled in the new grass under the spring sun
to sleep.
Sister otter smelled something delicious!
Coming along from her path by the river
following north to south, she came
upon brother tonkir asleep, his jaws
open, showing the seeds and flowers
he had collected for mother rordam.
Sister otter sniffed the fine scent of the seeds,
fat in their soft furry pods.
Brother tonkir had so much that his jaw pouch
overflowed.
He gave a great snore and food fell out!
Well, sister otter thought she would take
just one lush seed. It was right there before her.
She gobbled it up! It was so good.
It made her feel strong and happy!
Brother tonkir slept on. Sister otter
reached into his open jaw and 1-2-3
seeds she ate right up!
Everyone knows the food from the red land
is very strong - Otter was clever but greedy - she ate
more and more until in her greedy haste
she plucked two of the tonkir's sharp teeth!
And then brother tonkir
How he roared!
He growled and spit at sister otter
You have taken the food of our mother!
Now I will eat you to repay the food you have stolen!
and before sister otter could flee, old brother tonkir
ate her in one big bite.

Now.

Sister otter was in a bad fix. She was greedy, but also clever.

She had eaten the mother rordam's sacred food that makes magic.

'Oh, for a light! That I might see my way out of this dark stinky hole that is   brother tonkir!'

No sooner had she said the thing than brother tonkir's great tooths

began to glow - they glowed like the god sun but soft and white were their   lights - like the inside of a shell.

Otter held them up and said, 'Oh please, show me the way out of the   darkness I have found myself in!'

And sure enough the two teeth grew and grew, until they both popped out   of   brother tonkir - sister otter followed the great gleaming orbs out and

they kept growing and rising, growing and rising.

Brother tonkir was angry at sister otter, but they both watched as the   brother moons took their place in the sky, opposite god sun.

And that is how sister otter stole the moons from brother tonkir, and why   brother tonkir is missing two teeth."

"Is that the end?"

"It is."

"What's the red world? Can we go there? Have you been there?"

"Too late for questions. I was only asked to tell

stories....we can talk more in the morning..."

"Tell me another, papa! Please! You've never told these before!"

But he came around the fire, back to his bedroll. "No more tonight. Time for mice to be curled in their nests." He smiled and placed his hand on her warm head.

"Oh." Her tone was all disappointment, but at the weight of her father's hand on her head, she smiled. "Thank you, father."

By mid-afternoon, they had left common Tundin country, the staid settled provinces of barley fields and apple trees, and headed into the wilderness.

Fela, as always, was full of questions. What was the wilderness? Was her teacher in the wilderness?

"No, Mouse. Your teacher is beyond the wilderness, in Nameless country. The tonkirs are in the wilderness. We'll track them until we find a burrow with enough leftover resin to make a gift to your teacher."

She nodded. She was delicate and serious-eyed. She had his pointed chin, and his dark hair, but her mother's shape of eyes. It broke his heart to look at her sometimes.

"How will we find a burrow?"

"There are usually mounds of heaved-up earth. Always in the lowlands, never on high ground. Sometimes you can be above a tunnel and not know. They're in long networks. The juvenile tonkirs make them. They secrete a kind of resin that supports the walls. When a tunnel gets old, they crack off the old hard resin with their jaws and reabsorb it, and use it to build a new tunnel. Old timers say the older a catacomb, the more concentrated the magic in the resin; it gets concentrated when the young take it back into their bodies and reuse it, over and over again, across the years."

"Tell me again what they look like, the tonkirs."

"They start off small and naked and as they get bigger they grow a kind of armor. They're the size of a small dog, but lower to the ground, thicker, squatter. Big jaws and teeth. Except for the rordam."

"Are they dangerous?"

"They could bring down a deer, but to take down a grown man or woman, there would need to be at least ten."

"Are they really magic?"

"It depends on what you mean by magic. They work together to try and trick your mind. Like a game." He smiled. She was always asking about magic. Last night, he had to steer her questions away from her Uncle Pib. That was one type of magic he did not want to discuss with her. He hadn't even told Umila about the scrolls he and Pib had been involved with finding.

She said, "Tell me again about the rordam."

By dusk, he knew they were getting closer to tonkir wilderness. They made camp in a sparse forest on high ground. Alivar looked around himself, taking in the humps of gray boulders, oak tree and alder, the leaf-covered ground. A fresh wind blew. The light was still good, golden and clear.

"I'll unsaddle Rust and Apple. You go find us some wood."

He watched her head into a copse of trees.

Out here, in the wild darkness, among the sawgrasses, the cedars, the stars... away from the fear of others, he could still feel joy.

Soon, she returned, but without wood. And she was walking too slowly, her head down. The skin crawled on the back of his neck.

"Papa. Something isn't right."

She was holding her head with one hand.

He threw the saddle back onto her horse, and tightened the girth. "Fela, get on Apple. Now."

"Papa." She staggered halfway between Apple and the woods, and Alivar swung the saddle back onto Rust. The gelding nickered, and laid his ears back. Alivar felt cold sweat run along his ribs and he couldn't hear the nuthatches or creepers any longer; their nattering had faded like sunset's light. He hooked his hands under her thin ribs and swung her up on her horse. She scrambled into her saddle. Her eyes were closed.

"Mouse, can you hear me. Can you grab...here...take Apple's reins. Hang onto Apple. Mouse, do it."

Fela clawed for the reins. Now he heard low shuffling in the leftover winter leaves. "Don't let go of Apple. Fela! Do you hear me!"

"Yes, Father."

She only called him Father in the worst times. As Alivar re-mounted Rust, he undid the fastenings of his tonkir spear off the saddle and took up the weapon. Rust was pawing the ground nervously now.

Alivar's eyes became hard and searching in the light. "Hang onto Apple, Fela. I mean it."

"Yes, Father."

Had he walked right into a trap? Were they already in the middle of a catacomb? How had he missed the tunnel signs, the heaved up earth, the resin spoor?

"Fela. This is very important. What do you feel?" Alivar held Rust to the meandering forest path. The horse had started to skitter under him. Fela's eyes were still closed, but

Alivar saw her screw up her mouth.

"I...touched the ground..."

"And?" He was looking around, trying to control Rust. He could hear a rustling to his left. No, more to his right, beyond that low hedge of wild rose...

"I felt something hunting, a need to eat. A greater need to join...more of them. But mostly a hunger. Something wants to kill..." She tilted her head at her father, and tried to open her eyes.

"Was it like when you were with your mother? Did you feel something with your hand?" His eyes were everywhere, roaming, all along the forest floor, over the ferns, the rotting logs, the dark molding detritus...

"Yes, Papa."

"Now listen to me. You know I've told you were tracking tonkirs?"

She nodded but there was a heavier rustling, and Alivar froze and tilted his tonkir spear down. Fela moved Apple in a side-step closer to Rust. A low hiss came from behind one of the gray alder trunks.

Now Alivar could feel it...the insistent hum, on the edge of his consciousness, lie down, lie down, it said. Sleep, here on the soft forest floor. Alivar shook his head to clear it. "Fela. Do you remember...do you remember what I told you about the tonkirs? How they work together to try and trick your mind? Like a game?"

"Yes, Father."

Oh, it was back to father again. How big of a comb had he wandered into? How many around? Usually they hunted in packs of six to eight; why did it feel so strong here? Eight...Ten armored, mature tonkirs....

Fear was crawling out of his gut and snaking up his

throat like a metallic worm. He had missed the signs. Were they surrounded? Were they in the middle of a comb so huge he hadn't seen it? He'd heard about combs so enormous...

"Fela, hold on tight."

"Yes, father."

Alivar wheeled Rust, his tonkir spear still gripped tightly in his hand, and led the gallop for higher ground. He didn't stop looking over his shoulder until they had made the crest of the hill, and by that time it was almost dark.

They made camp again, this time in a copse of leggy trees on a ridge above a streamlet. Her father said the stream fed into the Naskatik, which they were following, roughly, east into wild Nameless territory. He said that a few days east from here, they would be clear again of the tonkir burrows.

Fela watched her father. His face, usually relaxed and spare, was tight around the mouth. This time, he didn't let her gather wood by herself, but accompanied her with his spear in hand, his presence behind her like a dark sentry.

The cold of late Spring bore down on them, heavy and cloying with damp as they unrolled their good blankets. They got the fire going. In silence, they ate some of her mother's jerky and nutbread. When they were done, she put the rest away. The smoke from their campfire curled blue, then dark gray, as light went. Even though the scare in the woods had left her with a tiny cold coal in the center of her belly, she could look around her, up on this ridge, with the wind blowing and see that the world was a beautiful and terrible place.

She pulled the blanket around her shoulders, finally brave enough to ask the one question she hadn't asked yet.

"Am I Nameless?" She whispered.

Her father's jaw clenched as he lit his pipe, then drew on the stem. He tossed the twig back into the fire as the smoke spread into his lungs. "That's what they call it now."

"What did they call it before?"

"Little mouse, this is hard for your father to explain." He looked at her, and his clear blue eyes seemed darker. "When time passes, people and events get blurred. Other people make up opinions about what might have happened. People are born with strange gifts that other people don't understand. It used to be...that Nameless Tundin...which is what you might be...weren't called Nameless at all, but were known as Enduil."

"Mages."

"Yes. Very powerful magicians. Mages who were united. They shared their gifts with others, taught themselves, and they conversed with the trees, with dragons, with stones, and some say, with a spirit world that none of us can see. The tonkirs were their friends. Tonkirs were sacred to them. In the old days, just to kill one would have meant rituals and other ceremonies for several days."

Fela frowned. "What happened to the Enduil?"

"According to the old songs, the Enduil used to have four Houses of mage-craft, just like the warriors. But something very bad happened, among the Enduil. One of their own people went mad...remember that yeoman-farmer north of our land? Who set his own house on fire, and killed his family?"

Fela closed her eyes. She remembered. "Yes. Mama said he was insane."

"Something similar happened with them. One of the Enduil tried to set...their own house on fire. So to stop this bad Enduil, the others left the valley. They fought a battle so dire that they were all killed. Some, it was rumored, went over to that spirit world they had found." He shrugged. "So...your mother sees one side. She sees that the Enduils' own evil ate itself, and she thinks good riddance. Others, like me, see that the Enduil risked themselves, the good they brought others, to destroy a madness that lies in all of us, not just Enduil. Now give me your hand."

He reached, and she put her hand in his. His words came slowly, as though he wasn't used to saying such things.

"Fela, this is important. I believe that all people carry a seed of good, and also a seed of bad. Enduil aren't bad, Northerners aren't bad. It's people, Fela. Not what they're called, not what they look like. You have to make that decision, whether or not to do the right thing, or the wrong thing. You have to weigh all of it."

She frowned. She did not completely understand. Was he saying she was evil, but she could be good? That it was her choice to make? Or was her mother narrow-minded? But maybe her mother thought that way for a reason. And how, if the Enduil had all died long ago, could she be one of them? It was confusing.

"Now, time for bed. We've had a big day. Tomorrow when we wake I'll move the horses, so they won't attract the attention of the sentry tonkirs. Then we'll go on foot to collect the resin."

She stood up and stretched. She shook her blankets out and found a smooth spot near the fire. The stars blazed overhead in cold beauty, regal and pitiless, but her father was here and she was safe.

She fell asleep and dreamed of a strange city in a steaming place, where tall towers with windows like eyes stood, and held back secrets. She heard their whispers, like a river flowing by in some arcane language, and she strained to understand, but the darting birds chattered overhead and drowned out that language, and she faded deeper. The towers' secrets smoked away, but the city held her, and held her close. She grew still and her own eyes became the eyes of the tower.

She woke in the flat gray light of early morning; a thin wisp of smoke threaded from the dead fire upwards. Her father was already up, moving the horses. She looked out across the low wild valley, where her father said the tonkirs lived. Then she packed her few things and waited.

Presently she saw his form returning along the path they had followed last night. She was standing and ready when he arrived.

"Now. The horses are on the lookout point yonder." He nodded to the north. "You follow me, close...do you hear? And keep one hand on that short sword of yours. We'll cross what could be a tonkir catacomb, and I want you careful and open-eyed. Understand?" Her father's eyes were very serious on her. She nodded solemnly. Together they set off along the ridge.

They had crossed the high ridge and were walking along the dark shadowed side of the open valley when the ground gave out. There was no warning. Fela didn't even have time to grab for him. One moment the earth was stable, and the next there was a ragged hole where his child had been. Alivar scrambled cautiously to the edge, spreading his weight out as best he could. Pebbles skittered over the edge, damp roots trembled.

He cursed. They must be right over the catacombs. He

could only pray that the tunnels beneath were out of use and old. After all, a fresh new tunnel, seething with tonkirs, would not have collapsed.

He stuck his head down into dripping darkness. "Mouselet? All right? Anything broken?" He kept his voice as calm as he could.

"I'm...all right." Gods, her voice sounded miles away.

"Anything broken?" He repeated. He could feel his own forehead breaking into a sweat. He looked up and around him, checking the underbrush in this shadowed place for movement, for sentry tonkirs come to gore him in his flattened thigh, his exposed ribcage.

"No. It's just...dark."

He'd left the heavy rope with the horses. That was an hour's jog away, at least. He thought quickly. "Fela, I'm going to leave you with water. You have your sword? Are you sure you're all right?" When he heard the affirmative, he told her his plans. "I'm going back for rope. You're in an abandoned tunnel. You're safe. But I want you to keep near the light the hole affords. Here." He dropped down a candle and some water, and his flint. "I'll be back soon, with a rope. You keep your eyes and ears open. Tell me you understand."

She did. He left, his feet barely touching the ground, his muscles springing and tight with urgency.

The young one had left the warm pink bellies, the breath of its fellows dreaming in sleep, to begin its morning. Soft-jawed yet, it scuttled over the dark hard earth and the belly ribs of the old tunnel to hunt and chase the rats who came looking for possible nests or a promising seed cache. Its eyes were dim, it saw as if looking through rain-drops. It raised its snout and caught dusty, empty air, no musk or spray. It tilted its ears, but heard no grating of hard-edged incisors.

Ranging halfway down one of the old outer tunnels, it felt a tremor go through the cool air. It stopped. The loose gray skin about its jowls quivered as it sucked in the telling air. A big thing, warm, some roping fear, a low smell, no tang of death, no dread foreign anger, but something else.

It paused. It waited, then closed its dull eyes and turned inwards, spreading the news for the other to see. The one that commanded, the voice that led and comforted. She came forward now, and knew all that the young one knew. Yes, she said. Go and visit this one. There is something here, a kiss of a golden morning. Softly little child, and go to meet this fresh grub.

So it did. The young one felt its direction, felt the purpose, stronger now, stronger than sweet grain yielding under flat molars, or the warmth of tucked tight bellies, the comforting curl of hip to hip, nutmeats in a shell.

Fela was in a brown, murky darkness but the cool earth was quiet around her. Softly the light settled; above ground she could hear her father's feet pounding away, she heard the birds scolding and calling and the sough of the wind in the branches. The birds were a comfort, and with this regular tether keeping her calm she turned her attention to the molasses-black tunnels to her left and her right.

Her right leg was bruised and scraped, her right elbow the same, but somehow she had landed on her right side and had missed twisting her ankles. She looked down the tunnel to her right. It was narrow, and hard to turn her body within it. She was a slender child, not thick, and she managed it. She looked upwards. The rend she had tumbled through looked eroded by the brown ropes of tree roots suddenly naked and dangling; water dripped down their gnarled joints, plinking into her damp cave, black and wet. She half-crouched, flint and candle in one hand, her other hand pushing away the cold earth that had tumbled down under the weight of her body. She peered down the tunnel.

Fear was a small bright flutter in her chest, but it kept her alert. She fumbled along the side of the tunnel wall for a stone, found one, and sprung a spark, but she had no tinder for the spark to fall into, nothing to light, only the candle's wick. Again she tried, and again to spark the candle, but there came a sound out of the blackness and she paused. Her ribcage ached from the impact; her nose breathed in the scent of clean cold earth, and there. The sound came again, faint, scuttling. She held her breath this time, and her ribs throbbed. Forward it came, then a pause. Closer this time, a gentle giving clat-clat of clawed paws, rapid, over the hard tunnel floor, and then nothing.

She couldn't sit up in the tunnel. She had moved forward a little ways and now was curved, not on her elbows, but almost. She backed up towards the light of the dripping tear she had entered this dark hive from. Her fingers curled around the cold hilt of the sword and she sat motionless in the sifting honeyed light.

She heard snuffling, very light, like fluffed cotton being slid in a box. Then that more dangerous delicate clattering forward. And as she stared, fear tightening hidden tendons around her guts, eyes burning to see anything in that dark cold emptiness, a pale form shuffled forward, furless, wrinkled, with eyes like glossed stone. There was just the one. Fela relaxed more than she thought prudent, but it couldn't be helped. The thing looked like a hairless sad puppy, except for the jaws. The creature paused. It tilted its head, and sniffed the air, pale nostrils widening and wet.

"What are you?" She whispered. Her grip loosened from around the sword hilt. This must be one of the juvenile tonkirs her father had spoken of; the young that secreted the resin for the tunnels and burrowed tirelessly into the dark womb of earth. And now she reached out a hand, but paused. The creature chuffed out through its pinkish nose, skin there moist like the underside of a snail. It seemed entirely harmless, and that alone gave her pause. It trundled forward delicately, and Fela backed up into the dirt behind her; she wedged herself lengthways and put out a hand. The creature then did a curious thing. It hesitated, cocking its head as if hearing some secret melody, and then it crept forward slowly, slowly, until it rested the overhanging flesh of its jowls on Fela's closest foot. Her heart beat hard, but she couldn't stop her smile. It even closed its eyes and sighed, exhaling hard, as if it had run a grueling footrace and the prize, Fela's foot, had finally been won.

Softly, she put her hand on its head.

At her touch, the world opened inside her mind, like a ripe sweet melon being split she saw the hundred glistening seeds inside, trembling with life, vibrating with creation... she was swept down a tunnel of light, and all around her a voice said, "Safe, you are safe. Come with this one. Come, come, sing the song we have not heard, come sing and we will give you your past in a river, a quiet river that has waited, the river of our lives, our children, my children. Come, and come. Follow my child. Trust. No harm. No harm. So much missing, so much emptiness. But the world holds still, vibrating, poised, quavering on the canyon's edge, all these seeds of hope. Come down to the river. Claim your lost world. You are our one. From death you come, a sign, a sign. Our most precious one. Follow my child. No harm will come. Let us show you your past, your future. Our hope."

Fela took her hand off from the tonkir-pup's head and breathed out hard. She clenched her fingers into a fist, but her own trembling had started, cold fear mashed her belly with flat teeth. But the pup rested on, not a care in the world. She breathed deep and opened her eyes. Presently the young tonkir lifted its head and looked at her. It nudged Fela, and turned, trundling back down into darkness, into hidden crevices and secrets. It paused again and looked back at her before darkness ate its tail.

The feeling, the intent she received from the tonkir-pup was sad and pure. And the thing that tugged at her, in the end, as she followed the pup down into silky cool black, was the dark kernel of longing, the wonder at herself, the secrets she could not know. The feeling that flung her out into the vast sunscape and made her ask, what will I leave behind, here, with my own blood?

And so finally, she followed.

The tunnel tapered down and it took longer than she expected, groveling forward on one elbow here, then one elbow there, through the pitch black. She could feel ridges along the floor. Then there came a curve to the right...were they heading east, now? Then again slightly to the right again....so perhaps south? And down. Always slightly down; she knew this because the blood went to her head. The tonkir-pup scrambled doggedly on, and Fela went by sound alone, following the scratching, hearing the thing's soft breathing, its foreign sighs and snufflings. The earth crumbled and was cool under her palms. The farther she went down the tunnel though, the stronger the tugging of fear became until she began to slow. The tonkir-pup's wet breathing paused. It waited for her and well, too, as the tunnel widened into other openings. They bore south and down. And in her mind like a shout was her greatest fear, greater than the fear of being lost or hurt: "What am I? What thing am I, that my mother fears for me?" Here in the gut of the earth, she could not hide from her greatest ache. But she crawled forward still.

There came a change to the air, a dankness arose around her nostrils, sweet with the fresh smell of water. Not the rotting damp, but a wipe of wind over a vast body. She paused, then wriggled forward with more hope. The pup in front clicked faster along with the pull of home ahead.

And then the darkness changed as well. Fela became aware that she could see the faint outline of the pup's naked gray form disappearing fast as the tunnel sloped down and away. As she came up behind where the pup had been last, she stuck her head out of the hole and a vague low light greeted her, an even slicker slope below, a widening out, a breathing in of the scent of water and more vastness, and dark shapes below her on a low sandy bank. She crept out of the hole, smelling, hearing, trying to subdue the wracking slam of her heart so that she could hear her death, or some other dark winged danger come for her, but there was none. She went forward.

She crawled out along the muddy slick and stood, for she was in a great wide-domed cavern, spreading above, ground sweeping down below towards a silent black pool. She peered. Along the glistening cave wall above the pool glowed pink lichen, in rough patches here and there. It was an odd candle-light to give. The tonkir-pup sat and waited.

There was a vastness here, a quiet unknown to her and she drank it in with reverence, for her mother had always spoken with the greatest respect of dark earth and the up-wellings of silent ponds. Even without her mother's hand to inform her, she knew. Its peace rang deep. Her eyes moved over the shapes near the pool, aided by the unearthly dusting of light. There seemed to be, against the cave wall where the pond's lip touched the earth, a mound, like a mounding of stones, or large pebbles. And then down by the dark banks, another lower form. Like the tonkir-pup, but bigger, much wider. Not a stone. Fela watched as the shape moved. It moved.

Fela sucked in breath and her fingers closed on the steel hilt. She backed up the slope, reached behind her for solidity with her other mud-glazed hand, but there came a strange low buzz in her head. She closed her eyes. It was gentle, soft. She knew, like a slap, that the strength of the hum could be much stronger, but it wasn't. The hum lifted into a feeling, a calmness. It did nothing to assuage the distrust she felt; that wasn't its purpose. The hum left only a calmness, like the pressure of her father's hand on hers. The thing, almost twenty feet below her on the bank, did not move. Fela's limbs grew warmer and the calm feeling flowed through her. No harm, it said. No harm.

As her eyes grew accustomed to the weird light, she could see, now, the head of the creature, and its wide back. Like a crack of silent thunder, the idea rolled off and echoed around her that this was the creature her father spoke of with such reverence, a creature rare, shrouded in mystery, owning every quality that was good and dear to the Tundin of an older time, a more golden time. This was the rordam.

Hammered by this realization, Fela stood and felt her grip loosen around the dull steel of the sword. But the hum never changed. The feeling never changed. Fela placed her sword below the tunnel from which she had come, and walked down to be closer to this creature, for all the laments, and poems, and lays of her people spoke of a rordam's great gentleness. As she grew closer, the creature turned and waddled back towards the mound next to the cavern wall at the pool's dark lip. Fela followed. She had never in her life expected to see a rordam. It was not covered in armor, like its children, or naked, like its babies. This rordam had a wide, curved shell on her back, like a shield, or even a coracle, a little round boat, with two ridges, like two sets of spines. t the back of the shell she could see the same whirling dark patterns she recognized from tapestries, or tattooed on the backs of women's hands, or painted on the sides of wanderer's tents.

Here they were now, in front of the mound of small stones. But Fela as she looked more closely, saw they weren't stones. They looked like crackle-skinned serpent's eggs. The rordam approached the pile and prodded the stone mound with her snout, then lowered her head. She snuffled and sighed, as though she missed something.

The rordam's head was armorless, like the tonkir-pup's. From its throat now came a deep snorting noise of insistence, and Fela jumped.

Slowly, slowly, the rordam shuffled to the side. Now Fela could see that the skin on the animal's short forlegs was sloughing off; its eyes looked rheumy and glazed. Fela's eyes had accustomed themselves to the gloom of the cave and now, as the rordam moved its head down, for she seemed to be waiting, she saw a small animal, like a little turtle, but without a true shell, crawl hesitantly from beneath the great bulk of the rordam. Fela's eyes grew big from staring. The tiny creature looked at her with one eye, unsure. With the other eye, it looked at its mother, for surely this was what this little thing was, a child of the rordam. And Fela saw all of the strange stone eggs and realized the others were dead, or simply never hatched.

The little creature crawled hesitantly towards Fela and the rordam huffed, and backed away. The rordam hunkered down and her eyes closed, and Fela could hear her labored breathing. The baby shuffled towards Fela and stopped. It looked back at its mother. The rordam pushed the child with her snout and the little creature gave a small phlegmy wail. The rordam huffed hard in response and pushed her baby harder. Fela...almost not believing what she was seeing....stooped, and picked up the little animal. It was cool and soft to the touch, its shell not hardened, its eyes big and luminous and sad.

The rordam snorted and backed away from Fela, calmer now, and trundled over to a dark wall of the cave that was in shadow. She closed her eyes and panted. Fela scrambled over to the darker crevice, a place where the tunnel wall slanted down. The rordam snorted again and Fela looked closely around her. There were more of the stone eggs on the wall? But that couldn't be right. They weren't eggs. They had imbricated edges like petals and were a dull clay color, as if the ground had been crystalized and formed into flowers. Fela picked one up, hefted it in her palm. She pocketed it, and the rordam nudged another one that had fallen from the dirt wall. She picked that one up too, and stopped. Far far away, from a distant memory, she heard a muffled call. Again it came, and with a great jolt she realized it was her father, back to find her! She had to hurry. She tucked the baby into one pocket and the strange stone flowers into her other and hurried, scrambling back the way she came, up the slope of the cavern, towards the tunnel's mouth. She turned once to meet the rordam's gaze and said a silent goodbye to those impassive, onyx eyes.

CHAPTER THREE

The Teacher

Alivar remembered the night she was born, the clouds gravid and dark with a late summer storm on the horizon. He remembered the damp weight in the air and on his skin, out in the lush courtyard of their home. The fumes of brandy, and Pib cavorting, trying to distract him from his fears: that the blood might not staunch, that he'd lose his precious wife, that his first born might be sent to the black mountains with her. He remembered Umila's rising groans, as the storm rolled in from the west. Then white hot threads of lightning in the plum-purple sky, and Pib pulling him into the great room, where his mother-in-law placed the puckered, pink baby into his arms. He had held Afelanua, and wondered at the wet black hair and the squall she made, the amazing starfish fingers, the swollen eyes clamped shut against the lantern light. As the storm dumped out of the sky, he had stood with his girl-child tucked tight against him.

And now that she was grown, and falling into tunnels, what could he say? "Stay here. Don't go. Hide. Don't do this. Don't do that." Why not ask the caterpillar to stay in its cocoon?

"What did you see down there? How far did you go into that tunnel?"

She shrugged. "Not far. I just...I heard something. I didn't know what it was."

"So you went looking for danger?" He made no move to touch her. "You're a young woman now. I'll not always be there to save you."

She looked away.

They rode until the sunlight speared down on them directly. They cast no shadows, trotting the horses along the higher sawgrass-studded hill.

The small strange creature stirred, turning in her tunic pocket. Her father's voice was a low drone. He pointed out the vining brambles of cloudberry, nagoonberry, sweetgale. She only heard some of what he said.

"If there's sweetgale, there's water about. We're close to the Naskatik, so that's good...sweetgale works for chasing the cleverer water spirits away..." He paused. He reached down and plucked a catkin from the bush. "Here." He stretched across, and pressed it into her empty palm. Her hand tightened around it, but her consciousness was still wrapped around the dozing baby.

She had said nothing about the rordam to her father. She didn't talk to him about the misty feel of the rordam's thoughts in her mind, or her secret desire to know who she was. It was as if she walked a narrow stone ledge, with her father's solid love and protection on one side, and on the other, her own secret world developing, forming in the dark abyss. A well of sadness rose inside of her, as she felt the old protections and comforts falling away, but with its loss also came a deep new excitement, a mystery in her pocket, a wonder over a potent secret. There wasn't the war she'd been expecting within herself. If her father knew she could hear the rordam whisper, what might his fear be? If he knew the rordam had given to her its last child, what dangers would he place himself under, for her protection? What other noose of sorrow would she set about her mother's precious neck? She rolled these questions away now, like a scroll best left unread.

All afternoon, they rode across rambling meadowland, full of the sameness of green spring grass, and then up and up, over shale-littered ground, a ridge of gray rock. Grasses bent in the light wind. At the crest, they paused, and looked down. Her father pointed.

"Do you see there? That darker line, an old stream bed running toward the Naskatik?"

Fela nodded. To her, it looked like any other valley stretched out for miles.

"Down there are the catacombs of the Ruby tonkirs." Her father began untying the knots on the tonkir spear that hung from his pommel. "We'll camp here tonight, but this is the most dangerous part." He turned to her and there was nothing hidden in his gaze. "You must do what I ask. Keep your eyes and ears open, at all times. Don't get distracted." He leaned forward. "You've been a good hunter, all your life. You're of age."

She swallowed, but held his eyes. "Yes."

"Sheathe the sword. Get your spear out." He swung off of Rust. She dismounted and did as he said. Her father found a patch of good green grass, and knocked a stake into the ground. He tethered the horses, then squinted at the low sun. "We're running out of light. We need to hurry." He slung the empty sack across his back and strode along the rock, looking for the best way down. "Watch your step."

She followed him off the rocky mound. They made toward the dry creek bed, then walked along it. The low light of day filtered through the leaves of the cottonwoods. Raspberry canes arched and vined. Crows called above.

Soon, they began to pass mounds of dark brown earth along the ravine shoulders. The creek bed bent and widened. They paused in this shallower, more open place, and her father looked around. They were both quiet, listening.

"I want you to wait here. If you hear me yell, you take off for the horses." He put his hand on her shoulder. "No brashness from you, do you hear me?"

She stuck out her chin and his eyes narrowed at that.

"Nope. None of your mother's stubbornness. If you hear me yell, what do you do?" His fingers hurt her flesh. "Say it."

"I run for the horses." She looked over to the cottonwood trees, still on this windless evening.

He relaxed his grip. "Right."

"Where are you going? Why can't I go?"

"These are outlying tunnels. I'm going to slither into one. Where you fell in earlier was too far out, too abandoned, and that was good, for you. But here..." he squinted his eyes, looking off over the wide, empty meadow. "I should be able to find some resin." Her father smiled. "I'll be back soon. And keep that spear close."

She watched until she lost his form in the trunks of the trees. Then her fingers sought the small quiet animal.

She tried to get the little thing to take water, or a piece of bread, but it seemed to only want to sleep. She sighed and waited.

Her father came back hunched and running, moving like a coyote-man, all ears and eyes, silent as his feet crunched over dry stones. He motioned to her to start jogging, and together they left the ravine at a high trot. The thought of enraged tonkirs behind them kept her moving fast, and soon they were climbing, lungs on fire, up the zigzagging path to the horses.

They made their camp for the night on the stone ridge. Her father was triumphant, exhausted, his face so dark with dried clay that when he smiled in the blue dusk, his teeth flashed white. The sound of Apple and Rust tugging at grass, crushing it wetly under the weight of their teeth, came to her. The wind was still down, and the stars began to come out again. She gazed up at them, her arms around her knees. Like the sleeping baby in her pocket, they held their own bright secrets close, and winked down at her.

Her father said, "You did well today."

She roused out of her star-dream, and looked at him. "I did nothing." She felt uneasy, as though her secret was a lie. It made her sullen.

"Nah. You did. You kept your head when you went down in that tunnel. You kept alert. You were a big help to me."

The sullen feeling slipped away into the dark. She knew there was no reason to be ungrateful. "Was it hard? Finding the resin?"

He blew smoke rings. "Nah. A little close. It's just a bit tight down there. Don't like closed in places, myself."

"Have you ever seen a rordam's cavern?"

"Yes, once."

"Do they…lay eggs?" Fela's heart began to thud in her chest.

"Yeah." He emptied his pipe and refilled it. "Used to be you could find the ones that were unborn, called stone eggs… in markets in the big towns, like Mok Taswan and Arrow's Heart, and out in Sealand. They're unincubated. Worthless. Some used to say that the rancid liquid inside could cure the cataracts if you gulped it down on a moonlit night and did a jig, but that's just an old superstition. People used to call them dragon's eyes. They said dragons used them to see into the future. But I've never gotten close enough to a dragon to ask the truth of that." He smiled with mischief. "Why do you ask?"

"I saw some in the tunnel. They looked like eggs."

He drew in on his pipe, then raked at the clay that had dried in his hair. "I wish I had thought to bring some brandy."

She went over to her rucksack and pulled out a bottle.

Her father stared at her until she worried. Then he found his voice. "Your mama would not be happy."

Fela tucked a curling tendril behind her ear. "I know. But Uncle's not here to get you drunk, and you like it." She handed him the bottle of brandy. "You could say thank you."

"Thank you." He took a pull at the bottle and handed it to her. She screwed up her face, but he insisted. "You helped me hunt. You get a share. It's tradition."

She took it, but the stuff burned and bit going down; it made her nose run, scorched her guts and the fumes seared her eyes. "Ayugh!" She got out. Her father laughed.

"How…how can you drink this?"

He laughed more, and drank more, then corked the bottle.

"It helps me think. Calms me."

"I don't like it. It hurts to drink it."

"Yeah, it does." He uncorked the bottle and took another swig.

Fela got up and unrolled her bedding. "Good night."

He tipped the bottle her way to return the wish.

She paused, kneeling beside her blanket. "Thank you for getting it. The resin, I mean. I know mama wasn't happy about it."

"Yeah." He drank again. "She wasn't. And you're welcome."

She turned over and pretended to go to sleep. She held the sleeping baby in her hand, and curled her fingers around it. She closed her eyes. There was definitely a teasing whisper of something besides the sleepy drifting feeling of the creature, a feel just on the outside of her consciousness. She held it for a long while, waiting, but no further would it give.

She woke the next morning to a fog. Water beads glistened on their blankets, on Apple's eyelashes, her father's boots. The bottle she had given him the night before was tilted against a rock, streaked with moisture. They broke camp quietly as shrouds of fog wisped around them, pushed by the wind. One moment it was deep and thick. The next moment, the air was clear.

"Ghost-cloth, my father used to call this, when the wind blew it apart like fabric."

Fela nodded, packing up her blankets, getting out the nut bread her mother had made them for breakfast. She wanted to be home and out of the shivery chill. She missed her mother's low voice, the smell of baking, even Ben's throaty warbles. But she said nothing.

Without more ado, they stowed their gear and were off down the path, into the swirling white blanket of vapor below.

By mid-morning, they had reached the end of the valley. The fog had all burned off. Her father seemed to lighten. They were almost out of tonkir country, he said.

"How do you know?"

"The rordam always builds her cavern as close to water as possible. The tonkir catacombs never extend past that point. We'll be well clear by noon."

They left the creek bed and rode through sparse forests of fir trees, cedars, white pine, tonkir pine, cranky bark pine, then over rolling meadows and hills of stirrup-high grass, through wild mascaris with their tight bells of dusty indigo blue. At mid-afternoon they passed through another stand of fir trees and came to a dark pond. Damp green moss covered the rotting trees at its edge, and a flock of wood ducks with their iridescent crests paddled on the water's glassy surface. Her father wasn't looking at the water, but Fela was.

"Papa!" She gestured. Her father turned slightly as the ducks rose and took soundless flight. But as they flew, they sparkled, shifting in the light, and winked out of shape, out of the air.

Fela drew breath sharply. "They disappeared."

"Mirage birds." Her father whispered, and his mouth tightened. "Messengers to the teacher, to let him know we're coming. He must be skilled. Either that or we both had too much brandy." He turned and smiled at Fela, but she was still staring where the dark birds had fluttered off as if through a tear in the sky's ether. A little chill of fear nipped her.

They rode on through rolling hills. On the ridges, the wind blew. At the forest's edge, giant columns of rock stood layered like a giant's stepping stones.

Toward evening they looked down into a low valley to see three dark round structures. From this distance, they looked like gingerbread cakes. Smoke even curled from one of them, like steam rising from fresh baking.

Her father grunted and they continued their descent. Fela began to feel heavy, as if something, some invisible armor weighed her down evenly and made it hard to breathe, to think. Apple's neck drooped, and Fela stroked the young mare's thick warm shoulder, damp with sweat from the long day. "It's all right." She whispered, leaning forward in her saddle. "We'll be all right, Apple."

As the trodden path brought them closer, the dark structures resolved into squat, shaggy-thatched shelters. One was taller, maybe for horses or cattle. The whole place looked as if someone had once had an idea regarding gardens and fences, but got horribly distracted in the midst of building.

A donkey emerged from somewhere in the dusk, and trotted up to them. Its coat was burred and rough. It stopped, lowered its neck and then as if in a performance, it tilted its long bony head to the side and a baleful blast of sadness squeezed from its barrel chest.

Apple stepped back, and snorted, and Fela watched as another shape, as squat and odd as the structures it came out of, made for them at a hurried waddle.

"Shag! Off you go, hie! Hie, ye greedy sack!"

The donkey batted its whiskery eyelashes at the moving bulk. The form took on detail. It was a huge, squat woman, old, with a heavy swaying wattle for a neck. Polished cows' horns were stuck on her forehead. A tattered cloth draped dismally between the tips. Her gleaming black hair was wound up in heavy braids. She was covered in a shift of dusty, voluminous black cloth, tied about the waist with a sturdy leather belt from which hung an assortment of bags and bundles and a small curved shiv. Fela was repulsed and amazed in equal measure.

"Kippy came down a fortnight ago; had a cow fevering with swollen udders, said there might be company. I heard the ducks whistling overhead, so I thought you might be near."

Fela watched the old woman, entranced. Rust regarded her like an old friend, and snuffled her headdress. The old woman petted him, as her father swung down. Then she heaved breathlessly and thrust out her palm in greeting.

"Are you the radthinar? Oliva? Alvar? Kippy, he was upset over his big babe. Never been one for names."

"Alivar, my lady." Her father's hand pressed into the woman's short wide palm.

"Ha!" She barked and turned to squint up at Fela. "My lady, my lady." She murmured. "I'm no lady. Call me Tab, for that's my name. But what's this? Here, fledgling, come down off that tired thing and let me see you."

Fela swung down, and the old woman put her wide plump hands on the tops of her shoulders, and squeezed pleasantly, then stilled. She tilted her head, much like the donkey, and peered into Fela's face. "Hmm. Hmm. Come this way. Young man, you take the horses in to Barley, this little pup will help me gather eggs for supper."

Her father took Apple's reins. The old woman nodded toward the stable. "There's old Barley," she said, "Don't be afraid of him, though his neck's a bit crooked. His people said he got his head caught in a syrup press. Gets inspired in the middle of the night. Runs about yelling, thinks he's got a war on his hands. But he's right as rain with the poultry. He takes good care of Red and Cackles, brings them grass, sings poetry to them."

Fela looked at her father, as the woman steered them along like a sheep dog herding errant ewes. Her stream of conversation, once begun, did not stop. Her voice was conversational, phlegmy, and preoccupied. Fela wondered why she had been anxious.

"Come on now, after you put up the beasts, we'll have some supper, nice eggs from Cackles, or Sissy, if she's been inspired. Duck eggs, there's more puff in their britches, makes chicken eggs look downright dainty."

Fela listened, trying to get used to walking after being on Apple for most of the day. The three paused at the barnyard gate. It was made of saplings, old and chewed through in places.

"You could sleep out in the stable with Barley but your child might be tender, might be best for you both to stay in my shelter with me. The bats go in and out, but now I've warned you, so they won't disturb you."

Her father unlatched the gate. He said, "We don't want to put you out."

Tab looked at him, incredulous. "What do ye think? You'll sleep outside with Shag to wail at you under the cold stars? But we'll see, we'll see! Or the barn, as it suits you. Both are warm and cozy. Lanky Tumor and Old Bib'll keep yer feet warm in one place or the other."

"I'll be back, then."

"Barley'll help ye! I'll take this one to the hens."

Fela watched as her father walked the horses off to shelter.

"Come along with me, wormlet." Tab began to shuffle past the garden toward the henhouse. "Just got some bulbs from the sweetwater creek this morning, not as good as potatoes but almost...with the eggs, and some of the old cheese we'll be good to go! Does your father have any of that Tundin tipple, the apple brandy?"

"Yes, ma'am. We've got some bread and dried goat meat as well."

"Very good." Tab stopped suddenly and turned to Fela. "And what have you got for old Tab, young woman? What secret do you have, simmering inside that young skin of yours?"

The old woman's eyes felt like wasps, crawling all over her skin, busy, seeking, but not to harm, not to take. Just... working. Fela's mouth felt suddenly dry. Tab's gaze crawled and tickled. Then she turned and continued the shuffle. "Storklet, I've got two talents. One talent is open, outside of me, connects me to the world, lets me help people and animals with their troubles. Healing it's called, but I'm not sure that healing's the right word for what I do. And then I have another talent. That talent is hidden, quiet, scares people, and there was nobody on this green earth when I was your age to tell me a thing about it. Great ram's balls, cutlet, it scared me witless." They had reached the hen house. One gigantic blood-red hen came out, purring a long low "awww," at their approach. Tab said, "Let's get us some eggs."

Fela followed through the low doorway. Her eyes adjusted to the gloom. Ominous clucks and clicks floated disembodied from the ricks of hay where the hens had already gone to roost.

"Why did it scare you?" she asked.

"The animals talk to me. Or I have the gift of being able to hear them. I have the gift, also, of asking a thing to take a different shape. And so too, other things, items."

Fela looked at Tab. "What do you mean?"

Tab pointed to the back of the shack. Fela watched, but saw nothing. Tab was motionless. Even her drooping wattles were still. And then, in front of Fela's eyes, a shape coalesced...gray and wispy like the morning's fog, no form, no legs, or arms, just a tear-drop shaped torso and an open mouth black as hell. Fela lurched for the door but Tab held her fast. "No. It's only fantasy. Mist from my mind. Can you do this, child?"

"No. No! It's not a demon?"

The spirit tore to pieces and disappeared in the dim light. Tab frowned in thought. "No." Now her voice seemed almost sad. "Some call it weaving a seeming. Some call it casting an illusion. But to me, it mostly seems as if I'm asking a favor. Asking a thing with some respect to turn into another thing. Watch again."

And before them both, a tree grew in the middle of the henhouse trunk twisting and gnarled before her eyes. It branched out and silver leaves flashed, moving in an absent wind. Fela stared. Tab spoke. "Can you see the pattern, the weave of the world? The roots and the branches of life's tree?"

"No." Fela whispered.

The tree faded slowly, like the shadow of the spirit before it. Tab bent over ponderously and picked a pebble off the shack floor. She held it out to Fela. "Can you persuade a stone to change its mind? Can you reach with your spirit into its core, and there ask it to let go of its nature and flow into water, or burst into fire, or take the likeness of a frog? Can you do that?"

"No. But I..." Fela's voice stopped in her throat. Again, her heart was racing. Tab waited. Fela said, "Give me something to hold. Anything."

Tab hesitated, then removed her beaded purse and handed it to Fela.

Fela closed her eyes and listened to the purse. "A gift. A parting gift. Someone...you loved, but...fighting. Oh... discontent, going away. Someone leaving. Your daughter... Mairin...death. A memory of death and a keepsake inside."

Tab was rock-still, staring at Fela. Fela opened the purse. A small dark red stone rolled into her palm. "Heart stone. It's called..." Fela grimaced. "The name of the stone is rube anahat." She opened her eyes as the trance faded. She poured the stone back into the purse, and handed it over to Tab.

Tab's eyes followed Fela's movements. She said, "Let's get those eggs."

CHAPTER FOUR

The Cricket's Lesson

The lady Tabita's home was built in the shape of a kidney bean, and in the indent of the bean was where a little garden had been planted. The arc of the sad little fence that enclosed the garden stretched from one end of the hut to the other, but it was broken here and there. Coarse hemp from multiple mendings that hadn't lasted dangled in the light wind. The small sapling-bound garden still had its bedraggled winter coat on, but here and there were the green sap-turgid shoots of daffodils, hyacinth, blood lily, and dog tulips. Fela followed where the older woman led, silent now, as they returned from the chicken coop to the home. They entered the hut, and it smelled strangely cool and clean; there was the dry smell of herbs, and the twangier smell of cat, but there was also a scent of fresh bread just baked and the homey smell Fela missed very much, of hearth and old cooking and contentment. Tabita motioned her over to a corner, and here the old woman uncovered a small dark laquered cabinet. It had two little wooden doors. Tabita bent and fumbled over dark shapes within and at last settled on a small carving of a tiny cricket. Reverently, the old woman wrapped the carving in a bit of cloth and pressed it into Fela's hands.

"Now you listen. Your talent isn't just any talent. If I don't miss my mark about you, long ago, your kind were sought after and taught well and thoroughly. I am sorry to say that those times are past. But I think this little one here will help you understand who you are." Tabita looked directly into Fela's eyes, and she tried to drop her gaze but found she could not. "I can't help you, my child. I am going to suggest to your father that he send you to a friend of mine named Heron, but Heron lives far away, and it might not yet be time to send you on a journey quite that distant. All right? But this little cricket here might have a story for you. So you take this tonight, or tomorrow night, and you listen, with that gift of yours, and see what it might tell you. Yes?"

Fela nodded, silent, and held the tiny wrapped object close.

Dinner that night was an odd, raucous affair. There were eggs and a plate of fried potatoes that, mixed with their jerky and onions, made a kind of hash. Her father presented Tabita with the sack of resin he had found, and she fingered through the gleaming shards on the table with an assessing greedy eye. She poured more brandy for Alivar and thanked him solemnly, for Fela knew now it was a dangerous business gathering that kind of a gift, and Tab was well pleased. The older woman looked up and spoke to her father. "It's a proper thing you've done, to try and find a teacher for your child, Radthinar, but I will warn you. My cousins along the

Naskatik have had some of their own children snatched in the last cold month."

Alivar glanced from Fela back to Tab. "I've heard nothing about this."

"Aye, aye, the Nameless tribes along the Naskatik like to keep to themselves and they're also very proud. They won't go asking for help unless the situation gets dire. But you should know about it. To be on the safe side." Tab glanced at Fela, frowning. "Rumors are that there's a bad man in Mok Taswan, getting a little power hungry."

"That one. Agadittur. Yes, we've heard of him. But the other...I thank you for the information." The talk turned then to crops and weather and while Tabita explained to her father about the journey to visit Heron, Fela's mind turned to the little cricket carving and the baby that slept in her pocket. Tab's voice interjected into Fela's thoughts and she startled.

"It's late, and both of you are probably exhausted after all the traipsing hither and yon. The child'll best be served sleeping in the hen house where it's warm and tight. Radthinar, you can sleep with Barley in the barn. Does that suit?"

Alivar murmured that it would, but shot a glance at his daughter. Fela simply nodded, and went to get her bedroll from the barn, her mind grateful to Tabita for letting her stay alone so that she could feel the little carving at her leisure.

Tab, standing at the door, turned to Alivar. She patted her broad apron down with both hands and her jowls shook. "There's no way to say this but straight out. That child there of yours is not just any little pebble in the riverbed of magic users."

Alivar turned to Tab, his jaw working. "My lady?"

"Radthinar, you don't have to be so proper about it. Listen." And here Tab's eyes caught Alivar's, and there was fear and hope mingled together there. "Your child, if I don't miss the signs, is Banwaduil, in the old language, Revenant, in our common speech. She can touch the world and it will tell her stories and they will not be untrue. Her gift is great, and I fear many, good and bad, will seek her, if they know of her skill, and what she is. Not at first, of course. She is still so young. But you must teach her, Radthinar. Don't hide what she is from her. It will end in even bigger misery."

Alivar's face grew very hot and his heart beat hard. What he had feared deep in his mind was suddenly very real and very dangerous. He thanked Tabita, and he did not sleep well that night.

Later, after Fela was settled in the hen house, she held the carving in her hand, and curled her fingers around it. She closed her eyes. There was definitely a teasing whisper of something inside, a feel just on the outside of her consciousness. She held it for a long while, waiting, but no further would it give. Then very lightly, her breath held in her lungs like vaporous lava, the bloom of a feeling spread in a slow tide through her mind. Shivering with excitement, she closed her eyes and let the feel of another world bloom around her.

"Little Will, God is just the breath that blows through us!" A voice was laughing. "We're only the flute holes; so you have to listen very carefully when the wind whistles through that head of yours." Here she was, as a little boy. She was in his hands, she saw through his pearls of sight. A man stood before Fela/Will in long robes. "Here, now hold out your hands. Goats again, eh? Let's get that off." Her hands were rubbed vigorously, but the man's voice was playful. "Are you nervous?" She/Will felt nervous. She felt like her stomach was heaving with nausea, but to her confusion, the boy Will just shook his head. The old man laughed at her/ Will and continued chattering tenderly to the boy. "Your palms are damp; I know you're worried. I know you don't want to let it show, but you'll do wondrously!"

Will spoke. "I might be a little worried." His voice was shy, a boy-child's clear piping, tremulous. "It's just that… sometimes I can't always feel things exactly, as my teacher says I should."

"Oh now, that's your nerves getting in your way, your fear! You've heard that from your teacher more than there are needles on a fir tree, haven't you?"

Will nodded.

The older man smiled at Will, a smile whose warmth broke through the lined frost of the man's aged face. "But you know its truth. Now, you'll be nervous, my wee chirping cricket, but remember…that feeling you have, once your fear is gone? Remember the feeling of how the truth of a thing flows through you once the nerves drop away? You just remember that, and you'll be all right."

Will began to cry. She felt the jangle of his nerves, like wagon wheels over a stony creek bed, before the hot storm flowed. "But sometimes…it's not just fear. Sometimes, I just can't see the thing, and then I get scared, and then it gets worse, and then, what if I can't do it! They'll send me back! I know they will!" The panic flapped about the boy's heart like sheets hung in a wild wind.

The older man's huge hands ate up Will's, and Fela felt him pull the boy close. His robes smelled of lamp smoke, and leather, and a woman's faint sweetness. "It's just old man fear talking. Don't you listen to him. You just wave at him, and let him go. Don't you chase after him, thinking he's the answer." The old man's love wrapped Will light and close, like the curling kiss of a rose bud. Will clutched the old man's robes and wept, and Fela could feel the two's closeness in the gentle touch of the old man's fingertips on the back of her head. Soon Will's crying spent itself. The old man dried Will's eyes. "Here, these are for you." The man went and got something and brought it back. She could see they were black robes, with silvery-gray embroidery down the lapels. "Your ma put on the old symbols for you, here, as your teacher suggested. They'll help you, Will. You won't have to go back to the tunnels, ever. We'll always keep you. I'll always be your old papa. No matter what happens." The old man unfolded the robes, and Fela could feel Will finally relaxing. "Put these on. The procession will be here in just a few minutes. And you remember that these people love you, and look up to you. They're poor people, with no learning like you've got. You've your talent on your side, and you can help them, with their cows and the udder blight, a woman's craving over a baby, a missing father...you just keep your mind and your heart clear, and you'll do well. It might take a little time for your nerves to settle and for your sight to work, but be patient with yourself. All right?" Will's father held him strong at the boy's thin-boned shoulders.

"Yes papa."

"Now put your new robes on. Right smart they look. Soon you'll be a man, Will, and learn things me and your mama could never hope to understand." The old man peered at Fela/Will with something like sadness. "Don't be scared of the big procession and the smoke-waving and all of the Enduil in robes. It's just a ceremony, like we've seen a dozen times. All right?"

Will nodded. She felt much better, as if a wild animal had finally settled down for the night in her belly. "Yes, papa.

Thank you."

"One more thing. Say who you are."

Will/Fela swallowed the nervousness swelling again like a sheep's bladder in her chest.

His father stood up tall. "Say it. Say who you are. Be proud of it."

Will swallowed again. "I am Banwaduil in the old language. I am the Revenant, born once in a generation, the leader of the four Houses of the Enduil. Born from death." Will sighed. "I name the world when the world whispers its secrets into the palms of my hands."

"That's who you are." His father watched him. "Go on now. Put those fancy robes on. Then we can have our good supper and be done with this formal frippery!" Will laughed, high and light as a bird's morning call, and Fela knew the worst was over.

Her vision cleared. The scene ended; the sense of the boy, his presence, the picture of the old man and his kind smile faded. She was back in the blanket, the night's cold on her nose like a lick of ice. The Revenant. Secrets in the palms of his hands. She lay awake for hours shivering in the newness of her skin. There was a sizzling ball of worms in her belly, all her winding thoughts warping in between her gut and her mind until she was dizzy from the spinning wild threads that she tried to track and understand. She ran and chased until she was exhausted, and she finally dropped off to sleep as the sun crested in the east.

CHAPTER FIVE

A Pirate's Lust and Three Treasures

The morning they left Tabita's lands, their day started with the dew of fog trembling on the gate, the straggling wild roses, last year's shriveled brown bean vines. The weather opened up into bright skies later that afternoon. Alivar took them straight to the winding course of the Naskatik. He said it was less wearing on the horses but Fela knew he simply preferred the river. Spring was still so early that the wands of horsetails coming up along the banks of the Naskatik stood with their dark bands tight, stiff as white-ringed spears. Fela preferred the river too. The smells, the sounds of the birds, even in late winter, were comforting. Once they went up over an outcropping and they could see the river stretched out, streaming east from the Chabbock. The water near the bank was oily black and curled with the wind, but far out from the shores it sparkled deep blue and the light rippled over it like a net of white shells shining. She watched the water so long it made her eyes ache.

They made camp just as dusk was coming on, along a sheltered turn of the river's winding. Her father said they were making good time; they might be home by the third night. Her father had seemed preoccupied on the journey back. He usually pointed out the water spirits' homes and the names of plants, bittergall and winter marsh and what they were good for, but this time he spoke hardly at all.

Fela had gathered wood for their fire and Alivar was smoking his pipe, leaning against his bedroll with one arm over his knee, his eyes watching the river as it ran in its course. She wasn't in the mood for a story, and thought that he wasn't either, but her father started talking, low, as if to the fire, not to her.

"Listen, Fela," started Alivar, "There's stories I haven't told you, majestic but historically important stories, that sound like stories but are for the most part, true." Alivar drew on his pipe. "Eh, I should've told you before this maybe. But never mind." He pondered and Fela watched him, curious. "Listen. A long time ago, the mages of the world and the queens…the rordam queens, were at peace. There was an abundance of food, no war, people were getting along, and art and beauty thrived. The tonkir tribes and the people's tribes were united. And one day the queen of the rordams came to one of the Nurs Enduil with whom she could converse, and spoke to this mage who could hear her words.

"We will help you capture magic's music, a rare song when sung together, and we will give you the gift of this rarest of endeavors. We need one thing from you: an enduil whose skills are such that he or she can hear the many voices of all the rordams as they weave their song for these gifts."

Now the lead Enduil, who could hear and speak with the

queens, conferred with all the other Nurs Enduil, mightiest and most compassionate of the magic users. And they decided that there was one young man fitted for the task, whose talent was for hearing the secret, silent voices and sounds of many things. His name was Sinda, and he was known as Sinda the Listener. And the Nurs knew of him, though Sinda did not know of them yet, and they worked their magic upon him and Sinda was drawn to make a quest. He left his home, and he dreamed while on his journey. In his dream, he saw a Great Rordam, the mother of them all, and behind her, in the shadows, the dark forms and shapes of great and terrible magic workers. This Queen instructed him on his path, and he went and did her bidding. For though his secret skill was Listening, his every day talent was that of a skilled craftsman. His work in his village and clan was sought after even in Mok Taswan, and even in the Houses of the Palinisars, southern and western. Now the rordam sang to Sinda, and through his Listening and the skills of his hands, powerful tools were fashioned for the benefit of man. They were the gifts of an age, born from the union of man and tonkir's best magic and power. They represented the sea, the land, and the air, and they were the Black Triton, the Drum of Calling, and the Flute of Life. These tools Sinda was able to craft, and each great instrument took several years to make, and they were kept at first, by the Nurs Enduil, on the behest of the council of rordams. The rordams advised the greatest and kindest of the Nurs Enduil that these were tools to be cherished, and used when the time was right, and this did confuse some of the less experienced mages. "Why," they said, "should we not use these tools right now, for the good of the people? And ourselves," some whispered. But the Nurs Enduil were both wise, and knowledgeable. They understood the great boon the rordams had given them, and the wisdom of the foresight of such magnificent gifts.

So the Enduil gave the Jewels to the powers of our country. The Black Triton easily went to the Attish Empire, in the Sea Realms. The Drum was bestowed upon the ruling Palinisar of the Chabbock, which united the Palinisars, north, south, and central, since they were prone to attack from the north and south; and to the Ringmaker's Council of the Tundin and the Nameless Tundin in the east went the Flute, to be shared.

And soon, many years had gone by. Sinda the Listener passed from the world. The gifts were guarded first with great respect, and then with great honor, and then with ignorance. Important ones knew of their powers, but the world had come into a strife of its own. Evil walked the land, and one day one of the Jewels of the Rordam (for such were these treasures named) was stolen. Only the oldest and wisest of the Nurs Enduil knew what a great calamity had befallen the country, and she warned her fellows. It came to pass that a young man named Finauld sounded a strident note of disharmony, shrillness, and discordance in his House and in the world. Those who opposed him were murdered. Good and kind enduil were banished, sold, kidnapped and destroyed. And the other Jewels were taken into hiding, lost to the world. Their help, when most needed, gone.

And then Finauld, finding opposition everywhere, and his power great, brought down the year of the Endless Winter on the land, and the calamity was so profound, so destructive, that the world was changed forever. Finauld found and destroyed the Flute of Life, for he knew it was the one tool which could bind men's minds and hearts, and wield the intention of many against him. Nothing could stand before him. But he was wrong.

The Nurs Enduil gathered the children of their Houses,

enduil, mage, witches, wizards, simple herb folk, musicians...all who wrought or used magic in their simple or complex ways were united, and from their deaths they breathed the last of their lives' intent into another instrument: the Flute of Souls.

The one chosen to create this instrument was also tasked with using it to bring Finauld to his knees, and this he did. But that is a tale for another time."

Fela's head ached. "I don't understand. They killed themselves? That doesn't make any sense..."

"It does make sense if you take into account how utterly powerful Finauld had gotten. It's one of the reasons, Fela, that to this day, magic and magic users are treated as less than human. But these mages laid down their lives in order to craft an object out of their combined magic...hundreds of souls whose intent was pure went into the making of that flute."

"That's...so terrible." Fela looked away. The thing was beyond her imagination and it felt as if a heavy dark object had lodged in her belly.

"There's more that you should know." He relit his pipe. "Some say that our lands...the Attish Empire, the Palinisar of Mok Taswan, and the Tundin...will always be at each other's throats until the three Jewels are restored together, with the Houses of the Enduil. But there is a great curse on the Houses, and strife among the peoples, east to west."

"What has this to do with me?" Fela felt the little Ota stir in her tunic pocket, for that is what she had named it. She fetched out the strange stone rose and slid it into her pocket without her father noticing. The Ota began licking the stone.

"Maybe everything. You've got a great gift, Fela. And out here, I can be honest with you. You need to know what's happening in our land. And sometimes you have to look to the past to see what's coming in the present."

Fela listened. Usually she loved her father's attention, his voice, his hands as he wove pictures from the stories he told, but tonight, so far from home, with more questions than answers, and still the strangeness of Tabita and the cricket and her own estrangement from what she knew her mother wanted her to be…she tucked her cloak tighter to herself.

"I know this is a great deal to tell you of a night. I know you're trying to make some kind of order to things. But there's more that I need to say."

Fela sensed the importance of the moment. She could hear the slight strain in her father's voice and she sat up straighter. "You know about the Empire of At, yes?"

"I know they are way out there in the sea somewhere. Many islands. Uncle Pib said."

"Right, right. Well, the islands of Atul-Orak, Alal Oranry and Alun-Akar were the seats of the Attish Empire; each island was one of a three legged pillar that made the Attish Empire. The Magersteres of Atul-Orak, the Portrays of Alal-Oranry, and the Elladars of Alun-Akar ruled the Attish Empire. These three legs of the Attish Empire had ruled the Sea Realms and all those islands for hundreds of years, but then the Elladars on Alun-Akar were wiped out by the foolhardiness of one man. Or so people thought."

"What do you mean?" Fela asked.

"Well…here things get complicated. Your Uncle Pib's grandmother was the abducted Elladar." Fela looked at him in amazement. Alivar continued. "Have I never told you the story? Eh, maybe I thought you were too young. She was the unfortunate target of a pirate-lord. During a trading meeting with her husband, Terane Elladar, the pirate-lord was dining inside the imperial compound with Terane and he saw Pib's grandmother. The pirate lord was so smitten that he vowed to return and capture her for himself. The pirate-lord, a red-haired devil from the North, murdered Pib's grandfather in cold blood."

"But...how did he get in?" Fela, breathless, could see the pirate's steel sword flashing in the candlelight.

"He gained entrance into the hall after dining that night under the pretext of discussing some last minute business issues with his grandfather, and the guards allowed him entrance. After he took Terane's life, he found Pib's grandmother's chambers, but guards had raised an alarm and she, Rianne, fled with two retainers and not much else."

Alivar stopped to raise the bottle. "Somehow...the story told to me by Pib...they used one of a number of underground passages built into the imperial compound for just such an emergency, and they made it down to a little-used quay. Pib's grandmother was very pregnant with his father at the time, but they managed to escape to a neighboring island that night. The pirates gave chase before the Attish fleet could be alerted. The pirate chieftain found Rianne, and murdered the attendants. Then, that night on the deck of the pirate ship, the pirate-lord gave her a choice. A squall was coming out of the north. It was very cold. The pirate-lord said she could tryst with him and keep her life, or tryst with the fishes in the belly of the sea. Rianne was beside herself with grief over the loss of her husband, and spat on the pirate-lord's feet. She told him she would rather swim with the fishes than lie with him."

Alivar averted his gaze from Fela's. "The pirate-lord raped Rianne, and then he had his men toss her overboard. Rianne remembered screaming for many minutes, for help, but....the waters of the Sea Realms are very cold. It was night, and the wind was blowing the sea into a froth of wildly colliding waves. She had no sense of direction, or space, and she began to grow numb in the chilling waters. She knew she was dying, and she asked her unborn child for forgiveness. After that, she remembered sinking, and nothing else."

"When Pib's grandmother awoke, it was a rosy dawn. She was inside of a rocky cove with high, mountainous sides, but the cove's upper shore was covered with smooth sand and it was here where she found herself. She was very cold, but someone had brought her water in a shell, and food, fresh shellfish. She was protected by a nest of thick dried seaweed, and in this way, she lived for many days, recovering. The cold of the water and the shock of what had happened had done her serious harm, but she did not see her benefactors. Then one night, when the moon was half-full, she lay awake all night long, hoping to see those who had helped her, so that she could thank them. She still had earrings, jadestones, that were very precious as well as a ring of her family's, and she hoped to offer the jewelry to those that had helped her. Early, early in the morning of that night, Rianne had almost fallen asleep. But she awoke suddenly. She saw a dark shape pull itself out of the water of the cove's mouth, and it moved ponderously. The moonlight shone down, and in the clear cold light she watched as a seal, one of the dark-skinned seals of the Sea Realms, shed its skin, and stood and walked on two legs. It was a young woman, with long dark brown hair, and almond-shaped eyes. She approached Pib's grandmother quietly, and Rianne spoke to her. The young woman froze, but Rianne could see that she would not leave."

"But seals...can't change into people? Can they?"

Alivar drank and paused. "Well, they're seal people. They

live inbetween two worlds, sea and earth. And these were the selkies...seal people...of the Sea Realms. One of them, a young selkie named Monani, had seen my grandmother's pregnant body floating down through the waves. She had disobeyed the taboos of her people, and had interfered with a human. She told Rianne all of this, over the days, with sign language. And she told Rianne that she would help her when the child came. Eventually, Monani's mother came as well, to help. According to your Uncle Pib, Rianne made friends with both selkie women, and pressed the earrings upon them, as mementos and tokens of friendship. They knew this was all she had to give them, and the three women became friends. Then Pib's father was born. Meanwhile, Rianne had given much thought to returning to her rightful place. But she had changed. She had stayed almost a moon on the island. After the child's birth, she had explored the island thoroughly."

Alivar looked at Fela. "So...selkies have their own kind of...sea magic. There are islands that are hidden, and islands that seem to disappear when one approaches. There are islands that seem to move, and a ship never can quite reach its harbor. Pib's grandmother was upon one of these enchanted selkie islands. But she decided over time that she did not want Pib's father to grow up a prince. She did not want to return to the Empire of At. She did not want her son hounded like his father had been, the possible target of murderers and thieves. What had happened had been too much for her. And so she asked for help from the selkie people. They were able to find a small abandoned boat on one of these hidden islands. It needed repair, but Rianne was resourceful, and bent herself to the task, finding and softening pitch that washed up around her small island home with which to repair the boat. Before she left, Monani, who had learned some of the common speech, had pointed to the ring Rianne bore that she had tried to bestow upon Monani in thanks. Haltingly she said that there had been another. Rianne had listened carefully. A man, bearing the same ring, with the same crest, had been left with a small chest on this same island to die. Thinking that what was in the chest had killed the man for he died shortly afterwards, the selkies hid the chest and its contents 'under the island.' Rianne could make no further sense out of the broken words that Monani used other than this phrase, but for many months afterwards, Rianne was deeply troubled. Her great grandfather, who had been lost at sea many years before, had been tasked by the Empire of At with presenting one of the Enduil's treasured gifts to the Black Prince. This was in the aftermath of the Endless Winter, when relationships everywhere, political and otherwise, were strained, and fealty of this kind had been meant as a sign of trust. But the object, the Black Triton, one of three magical instruments crafted by the Enduil, had been lost. And this knowledge Rianne kept hidden and secret until her son came well of age."

"Uncle's father?" Fela breathed.

"Right. Well. Meanwhile, the pirate corsair that had captured the Prince Terane's wife had been apprehended by the Attish fleet, the pirate lord interrogated, the corsair doused with barrels of fish oil, and all burned alive on the vessel as the sun set fiery red in the Attish harbor of Alun-Akar, the seat of the Attish Empire."

Fela shuddered. She could see the flames and hear the screams.

Alivar spoke quickly to Fela, the alcohol heating his blood and his desire to get the words out.

"We – your uncle and I – wanted to find these...scrolls. You probably overherard your Uncle and I talking about them. Some of them were in the Black Prince's libraries and we also had several – but what we realized one night, is that the selkies might have the lost Black Triton. That might have been the deadly magical object they alluded to. And then – well, we got excited – "

"You did something ma didn't like."

He pulled on the bottle. "Well. There might have been a little of that."

"And you and Uncle Pib…"

"Your Uncle petitioned the Council in Mok Taswan – it was just a formality – he wanted to go search the ruins along the Almenoc, chasing his tail honestly, he got excited about the Black Triton and then started looking into the whereabouts of the flute. He thought he could learn where the flute was being held, but instead he ran into trouble with the Council. He went back to his farm, and wrote me about… some worries he was having with his lands. But Pib and I thought – what if one could resurrect the three Jewels, Fela? The curses on the abandoned Houses might be lifted if we had those…"

Fela's curiosity was piqued. "Where are the others? Did you say?"

"The drum – it went to the Palinisars, but it was lost during one of the border wars with the Black Prince, The remade Flute – no one knows where that is. Some say the Spirit City. That's why Pib wanted to go to the Almenoc, he thought the Nameless clans would know. Others say hidden in one of the cursed Houses of the Enduil. No one knows for sure."

"But you and Uncle Pib…were you going to try and go to sea? Father?"

Alivar scratched the back of his neck and grimaced.

"Yeah, well. We're thinking about it. It's just that things are pretty dangerous right now. And then there's you, my mousekin, with her special ways," here Fela grinned, "And then your mother." Alivar's grin faded. He capped the bottle.

"Father. Uncle Pib…if he's related to the grandmother… of the Elladars of the Attish Empire….doesn't that make him related? To the Attish Empire?"

"You didn't miss that part, did you, sparrowlet?" Alivar put away his bottle. "Yeah. He might be, ah, related. He's not easy with it."

"I want to go with you!" Fela burst out. The sea had always been a huge mysterious wonder to her, and suddenly…she saw it all…the journey, the island, pirates and docks and ships in the strange watery landscape. She saw it all in a tapestry of bright colors, glowing mornings, long stories around the firelight of their campfire.

"Well. Well. We'll see. Let's go to sleep now. That's enough talking for one night." But Fela's mind was humming with visions of pirates and people who swam in the sea and wore a skin not their own. She drifted off and for a moment, she felt another presence in her mind, very soft, that reminded her of the tonkir pup but sleep took her and in the morning she didn't remember that at all.

CHAPTER SIX

The Attack

They got back to their farm late in the day, but with still a few hours of sun left before supper. Umila had come out with Ben on her hip, alerted by Brownie. Brownie, who had been Alivar's since she was a pup, with her scarred eye and one bad hip from an accident with a horse, ran down the dirt road at the familiar smell of the horses, yipping for her master.

Umila brushed her lips against Alivar's as was the custom. But she turned from her husband too soon, tugged Ben up onto her hip, and walked around Apple to Fela as her eldest child dismounted.

"I hope you found what you were looking for." Fela said nothing, but looked up at her mother as she stretched out her back. A sour mood fell on all three. She tugged Ben again, who was reaching for his father. Alivar took Ben. "I'm glad you're both safely back."

"Ayah. So are we. There were a couple of spots." Alivar slung Ben against one shoulder. Ben tugged his ear and dribbled happily. Alivar pulled the saddle-bags off of Rust and hung them over his other shoulder. He spat to clear his mouth of road-dust.

Umila narrowed her eyes. "Come inside. I'll get your brandy and you can tell me about it." Her mother turned, took Ben from Alivar, and went inside. Fela and her father exchanged grins and Alivar stooped to uncinch Rust's girth-strap.

But Fela stopped grinning. "She's angry."

Alivar took Rust's reins and petted the horse's sweat-darkened neck. He began leading Rust back to the stable. "At me, not you. Let's get the horses back to the stables, get them cleaned up and fed."

Dinner was over, the animals cared for, the children put to bed. Alivar shut their door behind him. But when he turned to face his wife, expecting silence and the shutters all closed against him and what he'd done, she was unbuttoning her work-shift. She tore at the thing with tight-lipped anger, but her eyes were smoked with lust. He pulled his tunic over his head. He flung it rapidly onto the floor. He looked at the low rough-hewn bed, the bedclothes tidy and crisp, soon to be wrecked like a reaped cornfield. He hurried with his belt.

"I asked you not to take her, and you did anyway." She hissed the words. He stepped over to the hearth, lit a sliver of fatwood, put the flame to a candle's wick, returned to her. Umila's hands worked over the ties to his leggings. "It doesn't mean I didn't miss you. I just…" She curled around him as he kissed her neck, her throat. She slid his leggings down part-way. "She's my daughter, too. Alivar."

"I washed the crucial bits at the stable." His hands went to the small of her back, and his fingers lingered in the sweet hollows there.

One of her hands ran down his belly, the other raked up his neck, into his hair. "She's mine, too. Alivar. Alivar." She staggered a little against him.

"Well I know it." They kissed, finally naked and home, in their proper places, and there was no more talking until much later.

Fela was handing her mother the bowl when she acted on impulse. It had the old sour smell to it, and for some reason she dipped a finger into the spongy rising, looped through the damp ball, and brought it to her mouth. She grimaced. "Bleh! It tastes like brandy…" Too late the words were out of her mouth. Her mother would have her head.

But her mother just looked at her, brushed her dark hair behind her ear and took the bowl. "Your father told me about the brandy. Hand me those nut meats off the table. Have you seen Manda since you got back?"

Fela glanced at her mother as she handed over the nuts. She shook her head. "No." In truth, Fela had avoided visiting her friend since she'd come back. She was still sorting through all she'd learned. "You're not angry?" She was hungry, and took several apple slices from the cutting board off her mother's work surface. Her mother's anger was like the wind, it came and went, and usually found its mark in words delivered with a spear of terseness.

Umila poured in coarse flour, salt, honey. The nut meat bowl clapped down onto the surface. "No. But you are right. I should be." She stopped her motions with the bread. She looked fully at her daughter. "You're a young woman. I can't stop you from being yourself." She resumed her activity with the bread. "Anymore than my mother could have stopped me, when I was your age." She murmured that last part.

"Did you do things you weren't supposed to?" The stone room was warm from the oven; on the table in the other room, Ben slept, for once, silent and tender as a soft cheese. Fela sliced more apples on the left side of her mother. She was still shorter than her mother. Everyone said she was her father in miniature, with her mother's stubbornness tacked on to even things out.

Umila laughed. "All the time. I'd go for walks with the wrong young men after supper. Drove my father loopy. I'd take my girlfriends jars of my ma's precious lemon curd without asking. I even stole brandy one night and met three of my friends down by the creek...you know your father's ward, Jeremy? He was one of them. We all got very sick." She looked at her eldest daughter again as she punched down the bread and stuck it back in the bowl for the second rising. "I trust you." Her mother smiled at her, and said no more.

Fela was overcome with remorse so thick at the deception she had contrived for her parents that grief flooded her like ice spreading its chill. "Mama...I'm sorry I'm Nameless. I'm sorry I worry you." The words came out before she could stop them. But she couldn't tell her mother about the baby rordam, or the fear that though she might be a revenant, she still didn't know what or how she might fit in. It might be that not even other Nameless people would even recognize her type of strange skill. Worse than Nameless, she would be placeless, empty, useless. Suddenly Will's anxiety swept her and she understood. Her hand shook and loss made her dizzy. But her mother's body pressed into hers. Her mother's hands cupped her head with no word. It was the safety of a lifetime.

"I know your father was trying to help. I'm not angry with you. When you get older, you'll understand." Fela nodded and wiped her tears with the back of her hand. Umila smiled at her. "Go check on your brother for me." Fela nodded and moved into the great room. The fire in the hearth blazed. Ben was awake and rocking back and forth. He held out both his fat arms to his sister. As Fela was getting him out of his crib, she saw movement out of the corner of her eye, down the hall that opened out into the western-facing courtyard of her parents' home. Her grandfather was asleep. It must be her father come back in for supper. She carried Ben into the kitchen. Umila wiped her hands off on her smock and gathered him up. Ben clamped onto his place at her hip like a pink-skinned frog. "Here...slide this onto the rack for me." They both looked up at a whiskery sound. It took a moment for Fela's eyes to register the figure. It wasn't her father. And she wondered, briefly, why her grandfather was dressed in dusty black. The eyes, though, were not her grandfather's eyes. For a moment the world hung still as a pearl on the tip of a needle. She caught it all; the embers like jewels in the fire, the translucence of her mother's skin, Ben's pink heel dangling by the curve of her mother's buttock...and her mother turning, and her eyes...Fela looked up, wiping her own hands. The black-clothed figure wasn't her grandfather. Her mother's eyes were saucers of pooled black tea and she pushed Ben at Fela in a sideways thrust.

"Run!" The sound that came out of her mother was like ripping cloth, a grunted scream, with so much force that Fela staggered back under the weight of Ben and her mother's explosive command. She pitched towards the dairy door that led through the pantry and out to the stables. But Fela turned and watched...still caught on that spinning marble of disbelief...her mother's body had become huge, a wrathful demoness...in one smooth motion, her mother had snatched the knife off the chopping block and the glittering ebony eyes of the man in odd clothing shone past her mother and at Fela; they leaked with searing madness...the man was coming for her...and her mother's hand was around the knife, and her mother's body was on the man with such speed and fury that Fela couldn't move.

"Run! Your father! Go!" Fela woke. Her mother's voice was singing taut with anger. The man had pulled a dagger....a silvery steel fish of a dagger...Fela saw the shining thing disappear into her mother's center, saw her mother spasm, her teeth clench, her face bloom in fury. "You bastard!" Fela backed towards the door....her mother's cotton shift seeped with crimson and her mother screamed this time, shrieking, breathless, as the man's body, intruding, out of place, forced her mother against the wall. "Run! Run! Ru..." The silver flashed again, her mother's arms, embracing the man hard to fumble his progress, stop his steps, had worked around to his back. Somehow her mother had stabbed the man in the back. The man cursed and rammed her mother's head into the wall. Fela turned and made for the dairy door. She heard steps behind her, cursing. She heard her mother suck in air, heard her mother's voice become weaker, and still heard the words "Run! Run! Ru..." The sounds still throbbed in her ears. She clung to Ben who had begun wailing in earnest, she threw open the back door to the pantry that led to the stables. She ran out into the cold night air. She stumbled on the hard ground, her hand clawed at the frost-tinged grass. She drew breath to fire her voice, her mother's voice still igniting her skin and her will to run, and run.

As she ran, she screamed. Her voice, leaking out of her

chest, felt like the weak bleat of the litter's runt. "Father! Father! Father! Father!" She screamed, and did not see the low dark shape running for her from the direction of the courtyard walls. She didn't see her father pelting from the stable. She collapsed on the ground with Ben wailing and she saw now, only her mother, her mother's eyes locked on hers, black lightning spiraled there in those eyes, her mother's mouth sewn tight, her back bent to take the hideous brunt. Her mother's hand, her soft voice telling the tale of the gift of water, the aromatic scent of a thousand meals spun from the power of her hands, the curtain of love like sunlight, golden and soft, safe and forever. It was an unspeakable transference. She heaved for breath on the ground, her mouth watering. Her belly bucked and squeezed. She vomited bile and acid, her mother's good apples. She heard growling, scuffling, her father's dog Brownie had locked jaws on the attacker's leg. She heard her father, saw shadows near her scrambling in the cold, falling, two figures, Brownie's body twisting. Her father's gasps....

"Fela! Run...the stables....run!" And she picked up Ben and began running, plowing for the stables. It hurt to run, her belly roiled, something was making it hard to breathe, the air like molten glass. She noticed another sound, pounding through her feet, vibrations into her bones...a third figure....in black, snatched her around and grabbed her chin. She fought to get away. Ben was whipped from her hands like tattery cloth. She bit the man's hand. He cursed; there was a stench of hot leather, and an awful smell of burnt hair, rancid grease. She lurched for Ben, who was screaming. She saw her father's silhouette get up, heard a low scream that was cut short, saw steel flash. Faster than she could have imagined it, the man let go of her, took out his own dagger, and thrust it up through Ben's small ribcage. Her brother made different kinds of sounds, and his limbs seized as if being pulled in a tangle of invisible wires. The man tossed her brother's body aside and before she could register what had happened or run from the man's blood-drenched steel, his hand was clamped on her forearm.

Her father staggered up behind now, and ran her attacker through at the thigh. But a third man, the tall man who had murdered her mother, came out of the pantry in the twilight, loping hard for both of them. Her father staggered upright, shoved his own sword sloppily at the man who side-stepped his thrust as in a dance, and the tall man back-handed her father on the temple with the butt of his sword. She watched her father drop like a sack of corn. The short man whom her father had gouged through the thigh pulled Fela down and though she struggled hard, the man had her wrists, and the weight of himself on her torso. She struggled to look upwards, at her mother's murderer. The man unwrapped his face as he walked up to Fela. He had dark glittering eyes, black hair, and a close-trimmed moustache and beard. She locked eyes with him; luminous hatred swam through her blood; the new hunger for murder made a starved spasm inside of her.

"This is the one we need. He cut you, eh? Clumsy." Her mother's murderer knelt and grabbed her chin. "Lights out, little bird." He raised his hand, and as her glare drove her hatred into him, Fela felt a thud and a prick, saw fissures crawling like crazed worms. The murky light in the man's stone-gray eyes fractured and dimmed to blackness.

Where was she? Her last conscious thought had been of Gray Eyes, and a stinging sensation in the side of her neck...she remembered her father. He was still alive! He had to be still alive. Where was her Ota? The little creature was gone; she couldn't feel her pocket but she knew the Ota wasn't there.

She opened her eyes, and in that moment of consciousness the new world settled around her. The bowl of apples going skittering as her mother's blood bloomed on her tunic, her brother Ben lying in the mud, her father's body, felled by the man with glittering gray eyes. As these visions tumbled by, one thing burned in her mind: her father was alive. That blow had not killed him. She clung to this thought with a lively hope that brought just a little color into her mind.

It was night. She could see the glimmering light of a campfire, and the low voices of men, murmurs of pain, and some cursing, the clinking of bottles. Her whole body ached. She was tied and trussed, on her side, in the back of a wagon. They had thought to throw a tarp over her and the knots were tied in front of her, not to her back. A boon, then. Her head ached horribly but she had to find her father. She had to get out of this wagon.

Her father had taught her knots and how to tie and loosen them. She started work. It took her until she was slick with sweat at the wrists but she kept stretching and working the heavy rope. And then there came steps, shuffling, men's voices, close to the wagon. Fela went limp.

"Check her, eh? That dart should keep her still way until morning." The tarp was ripped back and Fela forced her face slack, her body completely limp. "Ayah, snuffed like a candle." The tarp was tossed back over her. "Her da fought hard. Still alive though."

"Where the hell is he going, do ye ken?"

"The trading center in Sealand. Being sold to the pirates in the Makkars. Laddahamer's other two men left with him earlier for Mok Taswan."

Mok Taswan! Pirates! Fela's ears burned to hear more, but the men walked away, too far away for her to hear. She bent her head to her task. After a long while, she had just enough give to begin working loose the knots; she used her teeth and her saliva. And there were three knots, complicated, but all three the same, so by the time she undid one, she knew what awaited with the second, and the third. It took time, and she had to work blind, and quietly. By the time she had loosened the third knot, the men, who had been talkative with drink earlier had quieted. The moaning had stopped. The fire's light had died down, and there was silence where she was. The cold heart of the night lay around her, still and pressing. Then she heard something. She stopped breathing. It was a rustling sound, faint, and then something under the tarp moved. Fela stared as the little Ota came crawling out and wiggled the tarp off of its small squat head. It blinked.

"Ota!" Fela whispered. Relief flooded her...at least she still had the little creature. She rubbed her sore wrists. Her heart was beating hard in her chest and her eyes were blurry from tiredness, but the little Ota scrambled up her sleeve and nestled back down into her pocket. She could feel it searching for the stone roses. And she realized, for she had not thought too far ahead: where was she? They were in a part of the forest off the trading road, in woods with which she was not familiar. They must have traveled overland all day...not two days, surely? She was so hungry. She wasn't sure. She could hear the sound of a river, and this gave her hope. She looked over towards the firelight and saw the mens' huddled forms under their bedrolls near the fire. She saw the empty bottles. Carefully, she crawled out from the tarp and made her way over the edge of the wagon. She landed as softly as she could onto the hard earth. She was so hungry that she crept towards one of the men's packs and snatched it, then set off at a crouch towards the river's rushing sound. She needed water, for her head ached miserably, and she needed to think. She knew these men would find her, and kill her the next time they sought her out. She was on foot. They had a wagon and horses. She had to be quiet, and careful. She needed to get to Mok Taswan, and then somehow make her way to Sealand, but her first thought was to get as far away from her captors as possible. Her heart pounding, she set off into the night, towards the sound of the river with the pack. It was very cold, and though she had her good cloak still, the wind near the river bit hard and she was very hungry. The moons' light shone through the trees and gave enough glow for her to see a deer path that meandered in its way towards the rush of the water. She had just started down this path, the brambles tearing at her cloak, when she felt a soft pressure in her head. It was a comfort, and she clearly knew it was not herself. She stopped moving. The soft feeling flowed through her and she steadied herself. It was the Ota, and Fela wrapped her fingers around the little creature and closed her eyes. We go, we go, sang the Ota, down to the great flowing song, the water that winds, that feeds the world. We are near, very near! This way, this way through the dark bones of the forested lands! Fela stilled. Perhaps her brain-bowl was addled from the poison dart that had bitten her. But the Ota's softness became insistent. Follow follow! We will lead, it is good! And she realized: the feeling had the same presence of the tonkir pup...it was the Otal! Fela swayed where she stood. She closed her eyes and opened them and the world righted itself. Fela felt for the Ota through her hand again. Yes! I am here! I am here! I will show! Suddenly, a great weight was on Fela. She wanted to sit, to sit forever and not believe what had happened; that her mother was dead, her brother gone, her father taken Tun knows where, and now, this. The Ota speaking to her. She could sleep…she could lie down and just let it all go away.

No no! Not yet, not yet, the evil has happened and now we must go! We must go! There is a good place, a place of many places, a place of flowers opening and the knowledge will spill. Fela felt the gentleness, the incredible softness of the Ota's insistence and she opened her eyes. After a few moments she willed herself to stand up.

Fela followed this path most of the night with guidance from the little Ota. Below her, sometimes near, sometimes moving away, was always the sound of the river. Her fear kept her moving but at last exhaustion overtook her. The Ota led her to a hollow at the side of the path where the rocky cliff cut straight up, exposed by the vague silvery light of the moon, and she thought to hide there and instead to her great wonder, as the Ota urged her forward, she found the open maw of a cave. She crept in, so tired that not even the fear of a wild animal gave her pause, and before she could stop the little creature, the Ota had scampered out of her pocket and gone deep into the crevices of the cave where Fela could neither see, nor follow. The Ota reassured her and Fela could feel the gentle pressure of that calmness, but too exhausted to wonder, she fell into a twilit swoon and the day's horror fell away from her like its own bad dream.

CHAPTER SEVEN

Agadittur and the Cave

Fela woke up aching and stiff on the cave floor, her cloak wrapped hard around her. It was a dull gray morning and then all of it came flooding back...her mother's murder, her father's kidnapping, her escape from the wagon. She sank back onto the cave floor but then forced herself to sit up. She had to find her father. But first...where was the Ota? She fumbled through the pack she had stolen, looking for flint, candles, food. She found candles, and a packet of maps, but there was no food to be had. Fela lit one of the candles and got to her feet, and sought out the Ota.

With the light from the candle, the cave became a wondrous place. The entrance narrowed and became quite close for a long way, and then opened up into a great cathedral of a room. The light flickered and yawed from wall to wall, and Fela marveled. And while she stood gaping, she heard a faint scraping sound. She listened. There, over by a large boulder. Fela moved behind the boulder, and in the wall before her was a lower, much narrower passage deeper into the cave. She wiggled through this opening and the gnawing grew louder. She looked around with the candle in front of her. There, by the juddering light of her candle, was the Ota, chewing at the base of some strange arch made out of a kind of clear brown glassy material. Her eyes followed the line of the arch, and this room, while smaller, had a high ceiling lined with this arch, one side to the other. Fela stood up shakily. Hunger was making dark spots dance in front of her eyes and she watched as the Ota glanced her way (the Ota was getting bigger!) and then she resumed her gnawing at the arch. Fela peered more closely. Deep in the arch, she could just make out a milky shape, roundish, the size of a chicken egg beneath the deep honey-like gloss of the arch. The Ota kept gnawing at the arch above the strange shape, ignoring Fela entirely. Already the Ota had chewed a divot the size of Fela's thumb. Had she been doing this all night? Her candle began to gutter, and she realized she would be in pitch black darkness when the candle burned out.

The pack...where had she left the pack? She went back out of the strange opening the Ota had found in the back of the cave and sidled through the narrow length of the cave's entrance and there was the pack, in the wide opening of the cave's mouth. Why had she left it there?

Fela didn't hear or see the whine of the dart. Her eyesight blurred and fractured; she couldn't keep her feet under her. And instead of fear, all that enveloped her mind as the world crumbled was a white hot arrow of anger at her stupidity, and triumph that at least the Ota wouldn't die with her.

Fela woke. She looked around her. She was lying on a bed.

The fine linen beneath her palms felt foreign and cool. She realized she was in a city style bed, made of carved wood. She sat up. She could hear the sound of heavy footsteps coming her way outside the door of the room. Quickly she looked for a window, a ledge, an opening besides the single door but the room was dim and no other opening was visible along the walls. And then as she was sitting up, she put her hand back against the carved headboard and before she could control it, the sight was upon her.

A woman. Terrified, angry, trapped. A man – his veins coursing with lust, enjoying the power of a hunter who was toying with his prey. But they – both of them – there was some feral joy both of them shared. Fela was confused, because through all the terror and fear and exhultation was an alien contour to these beings' core that she had never before touched. It was not human. It was ageless, sharp with desire and some unspoken fierce fire and a word that went rippling through the male's enflamed mind...Urkhuska, a word she didn't know, and...what was this? Scent? They knew each other...by scent? Smell? That made no sense! She jerked her hand away from the headboard as the door was opened abruptly. A large man with a head like a carved boulder trod into the room. Fela's belly tigthtened. He looked like one of the stone giants from the wild mountains.

"Come." The man's eyes, almost completely closed, gave his face the appearance of a slumbering beast. The pull of his jowls turned the corners of his mouth down in a strange look of permanent discontent. Fela slid off of the bed's fine coverings. She followed the wide man down the hall unsteadily. Her head felt huge and the floor beneath her feet loomed so that she staggered and caught herself against the wall. The man watched her impassively, as if he had seen this a hundred times before. Fela righted herself and followed. He took her to a room where she was bathed and given fresh plain clothing, and the large man, silent, came and motioned for her to follow once again.

She was taken into a hall that was lit with sconces, and weapons adorned the walls. Fela stared at a scimitar's blade as it caught the light, and then the silent giant ushered her towards the center of the room.

A man, oiled hair pulled back, sat at the head of a fine table. The man smiled and sipped from his wine cup and though his mouth smiled, Fela could see no smile and no warmth reflected in his cold clear eyes.

He drank again, then rose from his high-backed chair. He smoothed his purple waistcoat of velvet. He raised his wine glass. "Welcome. I am told you slipped and were found unconscious near one of the great temples. Please. Join me. I am the Governor Agadittur." He reached for the crystal decanter and poured a cup of wine. "Here. Sit, it's all right. No one is going to harm you." The giant pulled the chair out for her and she sat down gingerly.

Fela took the wine. She didn't trust this man or this place at all and the man's cold eyes made her instantly wary. "Where am I?"

He laughed as he settled into the carved chair. "You are in the hall of the Hidden Fortress." He passed her a platter of bread. She took a piece and ate hungrily, watching him all the while. "Do you know who I am?"

She stopped for a moment and looked at him. Agadittur breathed deeply. And she knew, immediately, that this was the man who had so enjoyed raping the woman on the bed. And that he could know her, through scent. She understood suddenly. She paused with the bread in her hand.

"No," she said. The bread, though she was starving,

caught in her throat.

He sat straight in his chair and clasped his hands on the table. He said, "I am your friend. And do you know where your father is?"

Fela's eyes, at the thought of her dead mother, her lost father, began to fill with tears. She couldn't stop them. "Where is he?"

The evil man named Agadittur turned to the giant. "The bread is poor, Bom. Bring her some broth."

"It is already coming, sir."

The monster with the clear eyes continued speaking. "You know, you and I are not so different."

A servant arrived with a tureen. He motioned for him to attend to her. The steam from the broth made her face moist, but she did not touch the spoon.

"Eat," he said.

"Where is my father?" she asked again.

"We must work together to find him."

"What do you mean?"

"You have power, Afelenua."

"How do you know my name?"

"Because I have power, too. And if we put our gifts together, we can enlighten the people. We can stop such terrible things from happening. We can bring our gifts back out into the light of day where they belong."

"I don't know what you mean," she whispered. How long would this man allow her to live? He wanted everything that she was, and now she understood, terribly, and too late, why her father's desire to teach her who she was burned so bright. There was so much she didn't know and terror rose in her. She had to think! Scent, scent was important to him, but how?   He leaned across the tab

"Let me help you find out what you are. Let me give you a home. Is that not what you want?"

Fela needed to buy time. She was still alive, and there was still a chance, if she was careful, to find out more about her father. She hung her head, hiding her eyes. "I want my father," she whispered. She tried to flood herself with hopelessness, anything to stop this man from sensing what she really wanted.

Agadittur straightened. His brows knit watching her and he leaned in again. "I can help you find him. I will do everything in my power to help you…if you promise to help me." he smiled. "Eat now, and regain your strength." They let her eat, then, and Agadittur left her alone. She was ravenous and ate all that was before her.

In the morning, they took her back to the cave. The man named Agadittur wanted her to see something in the cave as soon as possible, runes he said, and by mid-morning, they set out.

They rode up the river and finally arrived at a narrow deerpath overhung with laurels. It took them to a mossy trail along the riverbank. The trees were tall here, and from each bank their crowns bent toward each other, forming a tunnel of green above the river. They followed the path over mouldering cedar needles where nothing grew on the stones but moss, and finally arrived at the mouth of the enormous cavern. Fela tried to sense the little Ota, but there was nothing but emptiness in her mind where the little Ota usually sent a feeling of gentle calm. The stone lip hung over the river, and cool sweet air flowed from the mouth, so clean it seemed to swallow them.

They dismounted.

Laddahamer gave commands for the two soldiers to

remain outside with the mules. He lit three torches, and said, "It's not far…it's through here."

Agadittur gestured. "Lead the way, Commander," he said, and put Fela between them and followed as the man set out, his torch guttering in cave's breeze. Inside, it was dark and cool, with the musty scent of bats and old undisturbed earth. Their pitch torches dripped streaks of flame onto the ground.

It was a straight line from the mouth to a narrow crawlspace. Fela managed it easily, but she could tell it bothered Agadittur's commander and Agadittur himself, but then the passage ended and they emerged out into the high cavern.

Shadows bounced wildly around the enormous cave. Laddahamer's voice echoed in the fitful light. His hands searched out a rough ledge where he laid his torch. "The first set of runes we found were against the western wall."

The light's glow became less erratic. Laddahamer strode to the western wall and ran his hands over the stone. "Here. It begins here. Look!"

Agadittur followed, and used his own torch to illuminate the runes.

Fela could see that the raised script had been chiseled out, line after line, and inset into a rectangular smooth surface, carved into the living rock of the cave.

Fela watched him run his eyes over the runes. His expression became hard and angry.

"You. Child." He motioned to where she stood, very still beneath Laddahamer's resting torch. "Come over here."

Fela moved her feet forward and emptied her mind. Her anxiety roared around her, but she summoned the incredible anger at her mother's death. It was like a silver pillar of fire that galvanized her, and cleared her mind.

"Do you recognize any of them?"

She shook her head and worked to feel puzzled, lost.

He clucked and placed a protective arm around her thin shoulders. "There's no reason to be so sad. Why do you weep?" But she only shook her head and would not look up into the man's eyes.

"There now. I only ask because these old words might help us find out where your father has gone. They might help me find clues to our past as mages." Fela lifted her head instinctively at the mention of her father.

She had to give something to Agadittur and she prayed that this monster hadn't murdered him. "Sometimes..."

"Sometimes what?" Agadittur whispered.

"Sometimes...objects talk to me. They tell me things."

"What objects? What do they tell you?"

She rubbed her hands together. He held his torch high so that she could see the wall. Fela closed her eyes. If she didn't give something back to this evil creature, she might never find her father again. And despite her revulsion, beneath the foul ditch of Agadittur's twisted words and malingering intent was a pure stream of truth, an honest curiosity that Fela could sense, and share. Fela touched the first line of runes.

"What is it?"

Fela could feel through to another world. "There are many here. This is a great crossing over place, a hub where worlds meet." She paused. "They are all here. Okol hol Dur, Banwaduil, Tamil Il An, Dreg Dar An, Enuil....they are here. They are here."

Agadittur went still. "Where...where are they?"

Fela's hand moved slowly across the first line of runes.

Her face had gone slack. "The place called the spirit city. This cave is the way. The river's voice will show the way. It will show the way."

She pulled her hand away from the wall and looked up at Agadittur with unfocused eyes.

"It's never been this strong before. It's as if I can see and hear everything so clearly. This place is like a trading route, or a highway. And I don't understand these words, but…this place is a shaka, and there is something called a hira…"

"A hira is the opening of the rordam…a shaka is where the rordam lives, yes, yes, go on, what else?"

"One must wait until the evening, when the river's breath blows life through the chimes, and awakens the shaka's hira."

"There are no chimes here."

Fela took the torch from Agadittur and walked rapidly to the opposite side of the cave where the odd sheets of the dark material lay stacked against the wall. "There should be a pedestal of some kind. It's here. I know it is."

Laddahamer fetched his torch from the ledge and began exploring the recesses of the cave. Agadittur did as well, and suddenly Laddahamer gave a shout. By the time Agadittur had crossed the wide floor Laddhamer had heaved a heavy metal tripod upright. At the top was a circlet of steel, and three sets of hooks hung from this circlet.

Fela pointed. "Here, and here. The chimes should hang from these hooks. It needs to be positioned near the mouth of the cave, where we came in."

Fela could see Agadittur reassessing her, as if seeing her for the first time. "What is this thing?"

Fela went to the sheets of thin dark material. She closed her eyes and placed her palms against one of the sheets.

There was silence in the cave as the two men looked on. She breathed deeply and opened her eyes. "It's called Lal Kiru, the voice of the river. It's a kind of wind harp." She looked from one man to the other. "The runes say that when the wind blows off the river at night, the harp sings the song that opens the hira of the rordam. This is when one world opens to the next." Her gaze went off past the wind harp, into the recesses of the cave. "Maybe my father is in that next world."

"Where does it lead?" Fela could see that Agadittur was trying very hard to control his excitement.

Fela again went to the wall and ran her fingertips over the raised runes. She tried to make sense of what she was receiving. "It says….a place…it feels like….the word feels like…a joining place….where real gives way to unreal, land gives way to sea….it says this place leads to the spirit city, the home of the enduil." Fela dropped her fingers from the wall. She rested her head against the stone and closed her eyes. She was too exhausted to do more.

"I see," said Agadittur. "We will wait until sundown then, when the wind rises over the river. Laddahamer, help me put the harp together."

When it was done, they waited. The day passed. Agadittur pulled on the cuffs of his sleeves. He paced the great room of the cave and ran his fingers through his oiled hair. Fela sat against the cave wall, so still that she was almost as one of the boulders that peppered the cave. Laddahamer had gone outside on Agadittur's orders, but then as the monster's pacing became quicker and more agitated, they heard it. A melodic sighing, and so faint it seemed like a memory.

Fela lifted her head.

"The river. The river is crying," he whispered. Fela stood up. The sound swelled in pitch and then faded, but then grew again and ran along the cave walls like many voices repeating a chant that one could not quite hear. And then, just as the strange musical hum rose to a multi-layered pitch, the wind harp began to wail, for wailing was the only word Fela could think of to describe this sound. It was a single ringing wide wail, and it sounded like one note, but no, if she listened, she could hear….two, no, three notes….it felt as if her eardrums were going to burst from the flood of sound that suddenly permeated the cave and then the cave became filled with a seam of dark light. There was no wind, only the sound ringing through her mind, but the seam was opening, and she could see the very walls of the cave dissolve and the seam showed light and air, and another place, another country, and the madman ripped off his clothing and in the maelstrom of sound he took to the blackness of the cave and flew to the seam, and, through the abyss of one world ending and another world beginning, he transformed in front of Fela's amazed eyes and flew. She knew then, the alien, feral feel to the headboard…dragonkind. The evil man was a flying lord of the sky, Urkhuska.

CHAPTER EIGHT

The Sea, the Captain and the Ota

Fela stood motionless, dumbstruck by the chaos of sound, as the dragon transformed and flew through the seam.

The cave went dark again.

Ladahamer and his two men seemed to be gone. They must have fled out through the entrance chamber. Fela, alone in the large hall, thought she could escape through the opening behind the boulder at the back of the hall.

She hoped beyond hope that her Ota still lived. She sat, huddled in the dark, wary and alert, and then there came a snuffling. The little Ota crawled slowly up her sleeve. By its silence and its movement she knew it was very tired. Fela, greatly relieved to find her alive, petted the small creature gently and waited as the Ota chewed diligently on the stone rose.

For a long time she waited, but no one came. Finally, Fela

crept out, her joints stiff from being still for so long. The men had left behind packs with some food and candles. She struck a flame, and ate a little. She shivered. The cave was cold, and damp. But the runes...the runes had spoken to her, the walls had given her voice.

She was trying to understand the difference between what she learned from touching human skin, and what the inscriptions had given her.

When she touched another person, it felt like the pressure of a grip of several fingers. If she could follow that pressure, it brought texture, emotions, artifacts of feeling that flowed through her mind and sent tentacles into her gut and out her arms. The feeling was deep and carried colorful cells of information - the heart's longing, the feel of a dead rabbit's pelt, the wind at the nape of the neck. She was learning to sift and mine through this strange coinage, to sequester away her own rising fear or burgeoning joy at another's strong surge of emotion - to catalogue the shades of feeling, thought, sound, visions that dazzled...it all landed in a tumultuous pile. It was difficult to separate her own fears from the fears of another, but she was learning to sort through the odd treasure, and make sense of it. But the stone inscriptions had been different.

The carver had imparted the meaning clearly. But behind the hard clarity of the stone were shadows, tendrils of feeling, moments of events, and these teased around the edges of her awareness like silvery wasps. As if the two feelings...the hard of stone and the shadow of something else...were not related. But how could she bring the shadow into focus?

She sighed and shook her head. It was beyond her for the moment. The Ota had disappeared again. Fela could hear her chewing. She followed her with the light, then stopped and stared. The Ota had succeeded in chewing a roundish hole through the glossy arch and there, at the base, had landed three rocks, freed from their encasement in the arch.

She hefted one. It had a gray stony exterior, but was shaped like an egg. It was heavy. She closed her eyes and tried to feel the egg. Nothing.

She was cramped and tired and ready at last to dare venturing out. She gathered up the Ota and the strange eggs, shouldered one of the packs with food, and left the cave.

She followed the deer path back to the main trading route. She thought she could go to her Uncle Pib's lands and get help, but she could feel, viscerally, that Agadittur would hunt her to the ends of the earth. She knew this as a deer knows they are prey. Even now, she could feel Agadittur's cold eyes burning into hers; she had something he desperately wanted and he would stop at nothing to reclaim her. How could she bring this on her father's best friend? And her father. The longer she tarried, safe and warm, on somebody else's property, the more likely it was that her father would be lost to her forever. No.

As night fell, she huddled in the stables of a roadside inn. In the dark, she thought. The harder path lay not in seeking help, but in going alone, right through to Sealand. Days had already been lost, and she would have to hurry to get there at the same time as her father and her captors.

The next day, she trudged the main trading route that led first to Arrow's Heart. That evening, she met up with a band of itinerant pickers whose job it was to gather leaves on which a certain kind of insect had secreted a resin. The resin was hallucinogenic and highly prized in trade. Fela cooked for them that night, and after several days left with two silver coins in her pocket and provisions in her pack.

On the outskirts of Sealand, at a market in Tanbark Bay, a cheerful family let her ride in their wagon. She told them she was going to find her uncle. They crossed a great wooden bridge over an enormous lake. The bridge, as wide as a road, was supported on pillars sunk in the black waters of the lake, and Fela marveled.

Now they were almost in the city. The farmer's wife pressed a cloth-covered cheese into Fela's hands, and then the wagon was creaking off and away down the road. Fela waved as the farmer's wife looked back once in bland concern, and then they were lost in the traffic of the bright morning and Fela stood, alone in the winter sun. She shouldered her pack, and joined the other travelers.

Girls on mules carried sacks of unspun wool. There were herbalists with their bundles of dried flowers and roots, tanners with wagons of skins and shepherds driving young lambs and goats. A kid clattered past Fela crying for its mother. It was crowded, the road was muddy, but people were cheery and polite. The sun was glorious, and everyone's temperaments profited from the gentler weather.

As the road took a turn Fela could see row upon row of stout stone buildings. There were taverns, a forge, mercantile shops. The road led along a gentle ridge, and she could see, far below, the astonishing sight of the shining sea.

The sunlight glittered and darted over the water. Great sea-going vessels sat moored in the bay, far out over the dark stretch of water. Smaller boats were tied along the docks and quays. She took in the strange marsh tang scent of the sea, the great full bellies of the ships setting sail...she was mesmerized. Then she remembered herself. What should she do?

Even if she got to the trading center, and found her father, how was she to rescue him? What good would it be to have come this far, only to learn her father had already been sold to ruthless pirates?

There had to be a way. Maybe if she knew the names of ships that took slaves, she could get work somehow…but as a young woman?

She closed her eyes and tried not to despair. She steeled herself and decided to try at the red roofed inn behind her.

Fela stepped through the wide doors of the hostelry into a bright, pine-lined room. There were purple flowers in a clay vase. A black and white cat sauntered by. A woman was working at papers and at the sight of Fela she put down her pen. "Well, and what have we here? Child, where's your family?"

Fela hoisted her pack, and told the same lie she had been telling others on the road. "I'm supposed to meet my uncle at the trading center. Where they…where slaves are sold to the pirates of the Makkars."

The woman's head tilted and she stared at Fela. Fela began to grow hot. The woman came from around the counter. She wore long skirts of dark blue and she frowned formidably. "Your uncle is at the trading center? Why?"

"He's taking me to…to try and seek my father! My father was kidnapped, unjustly!" She didn't mean to say those words. It was all suddenly too much, and everything blurred together, the farmer's wife, the maddas pickers, the cave, the dragon, little Ben, her mother's murder, and her head felt too big…the room juddered sharply down and the next thing she knew she was on a divan with the innkeeper hovering over her.

"Child. Can you hear me?" The woman was rubbing her

hands. The woman's hands were so warm. Fela shuddered, not realizing how cold she was.

"What happened?"

"You fainted dead away. Now listen. Lie here, and I'll bring you a bite to eat."

Fela looked around warily. There was no one else in the room. She lay back.

The woman came bustling in with bread, cheese and fruit. "Here you are. Poor thing. What's your name?"

"Anua. An, for short."

"Well, An, you gave me quite a start. I'm Blinny. This is my inn."

Fela sat up as Blinny set the plate of food in her lap. "You're Tundin, yes? You look worn out. The dark circles under your eyes! Tell me everything, and I'll try to help."

The apple was wrinkled, but still sweet and delicious. Fela ate, and told Blinny the important parts, but left out names. She didn't know what else to do and she hadn't realized how tired she was. The food refreshed her and Blinny's kind attention beguiled her heart.

"Now you listen to me. I still keep my eyes on the captains and the ships. Many of my friends are sea-going. You don't want to be messing about at the trading center. That's a right dangerous place. What you want is the ship! And you're right about one thing. The Makkars are where there's a brisk trade in black market slaves and that's where the Attish pirates and the southern pirates, the Red Cape pirates and the other ne'er do wells go to sell and buy goods, including slaves.

"The three ships currently working with the pirates are the Farland, the Gunnery, and the Stoutheart. Now I happen to know that the Gunnery and the Stoutheart aren't in port right now, so that leaves the Farland. She's out in the bay and her captain is Captain Carles. They call him the Curlew, but don't call him that if you want to stay on his good side. He'll tell you if he's transporting slaves. Here."

Blinny got up and bustled to her writing counter, wrote something on a piece of paper, rolled it up and secured it, and handed it to Fela. "This will help. I know old Curlew and this'll make him be honest with you. A young girl like you, and all. Looking for your kidnapped father. What has this world come to."

Fela tucked the parchment inside her cloak and thanked Blinny. She ate the bread and cheese and felt better, but her shame at fainting...she wanted to leave. It was safe at the inn, but she had to find her father, and she needed to get to the Farland before the sun set. Already it was lowering in the sky.

Fela thanked Blinny again and took out one of the silver coins, but Blinny shook her head vigorously. "You go find your father, and come back here. I'll give you a room for the night and then we'll discuss coins. You just mind yourself, and don't go to the trading center! Head to the docks at the market place along the waterfront. You'll see the Farland tied up. Tun go with you, child."

Fela left the kindness of Blinny and walked out into the cold bright day. The way down to the docks and piers was magnificent and bewildering. She had grown up with the idea of the sea, but the nearness of it all...the shipmakers hammering, the sailors shouting to each other in languages she'd never heard. There were shops and houses with cut stone foundations and white washed clapboard sides, bleached from weather. She saw netting shops, caulkers and sailmakers. In the marketplace, clamsellers sang out their wares and row upon row of wooden cases stood filled with silver fish and pink tentacled creatures. And all the ships! There were two tied up close: Fela stopped a sailor striding by with a load. He grunted and pointed to the Farland.

The master of that vessel, a great man in a long red coat, stood pointing and yelling while men ran around with ropes, sails, boxes of tools and great heaps of goods. A smaller man in a black tunic down to his knees stood by his side. As Fela approached she saw the man bend the captain's head in whispered talk.

Fela steeled herself and moved forward.

"Are you the weather worker that Elm sent? Great Tun of the Open Sea!! And so young a woman! Ha!" The captain gave a great bark of a laugh and Fela smiled despite herself, for the laugh was full of mirth. Composing herself, she addressed the captain.

"I am sent by no one named Elm, sir. I was referred to you..."

Captain Carles cut her off. "I just need to know one thing, little duck! Can you call the winds?"

Fela started. "No, I..."

"Then what good are you, Elm be damned!" The captain threw up his hands, and strode from her and made for the smaller man and here the two conversed quietly, the slighter man's dark eyes appraising her beadily. Fela waited. The Captain approached her again. "Well, my man here says you are a dab hand at magery, sure as he's one himself. So what's your skill? You can't call the winds, but sure Elm has sent you, so what is it you can do? Can you raise a fog to hide my craft, or bewitch the oars? Can you tell cheat from honest?"

"I can't do any of the others...but..."

"What good are ye, then! Get the witch off the ship, Moldock."

"Wait! I…I can tell cheat from honest. I can do that! But Captain…"

He turned to her, frowning. "Aye?"

"I wasn't…I mean Elm didn't send me. I'm looking for my father. He was kidnapped, and sold, so I have been told, and I was also told one of three ships would've taken him…"

The captain frowned. "Who told you all this, then?"

Fela handed the captain Blinny's parchment. He opened it and read, and some of the irritated lines in his face smoothed.

"Well, Blinny. A soft touch, but a good heart. Didn't know what you were, though, did she! But there's been an odd wrinkle. The shipment of slaves was taken by the Gunnery a day too soon, and we're to set sail tonight, on the outgoing tide, to meet her in the Chains. Tell you what, I'll give you passage if you'll just run your eye over the new crew."

Fela hesitantly looked at the crewmen, twenty or so, who hunched over great coils of rope, or picked their teeth, or stood eyeing her suspiciously. She said, "I need to touch them."

"Touch them?"

"Yes. Their hands. I can…shake their hands."

The captain rolled his shoulders and gestured to the thin man in the black tunic. "Moldock! Help her!" and the captain strode off.

Fela went through each sailor, and nodded or shook her head as the crewmen revealed themselves to her. Most were petty thieves, reformed to sailoring. She put to use all the skill she'd learned that helped her separate her feelings from theirs. Some were so addled by drink she got nothing coherent from them, but they weren't evil or given to stealing. Most were lonely and craved the sea. Two were so dangerous that touching them made her catch her breath. Killing, to both of these men, was an offhand thing, like drinking water or opening a door.

She told Moldock, who dismissed them quickly. As they left, they scowled back at her.

That night on the ebb tide, the Farland weighed anchor and rode out of the bay. Fela was given the cabin boy's bunk, as he had taken sick and was off the ship. Later that evening, Moldock fetched her, and left her before the captain's open door.

"Come in, Anua."

She went forward. His office was dark wood, lit by a lantern. Smoke curled from a pipe on a clay dish. Papers and maps and odd brass tools gleamed in the lamplight on his desk. "Come. I want to give you this."

He took a gold coin from his coat vest and tossed it onto the desk. "One of the men you steered me away from had a warrant on his head. Moldock collected the reward before we sailed this evening. I thank you for that."

Fela tried to keep her face still as she tucked the gold coin away, but alarms were ringing in her head, her heart. She stepped around the desk and looked at the map that the captain's hands kept open and flat to the table. He used one of the tools to hold it down and moved a finger towards a group of islands. "You have letters? Good. Then you can cipher the names of these islands. We're here, see? Up in this harbor for the night. Aptly named Midnight Harbor." The captain smiled. "We were supposed to set sail for the Makkars." He pointed on the map, and Fela read names like Pinjab, Skull, Fingerlock. There were more islands, perhaps twelve in all, but the writing was very small. "But my orders have changed. We're going to Tanlaysing instead." He took his other hand off the map and it rolled back into a tube.

Her alarm turned suddenly to anger and hopelessness and she could not stop her voice. "My father will be sold! I'll never see him again! You promised me passage, you told me…"

"I'm going to tell you a good thing," the captain interrupted. "Your father. Even if he's there at Worhag, as merchandise, and I doubt it, it will cost you 50 gold pieces at the least to buy him from the pirates." The captain looked squarely at her, his eyes glinting in the lanternlight. "Do you have 50 gold pieces? No?" he smiled. Fela's heart was beating high and hard in her chest, making her throat feel blocked. The only thing in the world she wanted, that she had to do, was find her father. "I give you an opportunity. I will let you work for me for one piece of silver a week; a palinisar's ransom. How many Nameless witches can say they earn a fair wage? Stay on my ship and help me tell bad business from good, and in a year or so, you can earn enough to buy your father back. If you can track him down."

The captain smiled and there was no joy or mirth now in the smile.

Fela was in a red storm of anger, but in her mind the Ota was suddenly pressing. It is good. They are coming. They are coming.

Fela blinked rapidly, trying to clear her eyes, her mind. "I did everything you asked! I've earned my passage to the place… Worhag…where my father is going to be sold! You must take me there!" She tried to rein in her heat, to breathe in, the way her mother had taught her when her temper flared. The captain watched her with amused eyes. The Ota sang, All will be well. All will be well. Great acts will unfold. What is missing was never lost.

The Ota's words were confusing but somehow soothed her mind enough to clear. The truth came to her.

"You were never bound for Worhag, were you? You lied to me from the start."

"You're a quick one." The captain's hands covered his expansive belly. "It's a two day trip to Tanlaysing. Then back to Sealand. During our voyage, you can consider the course laid before you." The captain smiled again. "I hope you choose wisely."

Fela walked back to the tiny bunkroom and fell onto the pallet in the darkness. It smelled like mold and fish oil in the cabin and her heart spilled over. The Ota reassured and sang, over and over, that all was well, but Fela wept and raged silently into the dark room.

She awoke suddenly, thrust into the wall of the cabin by the rolling of the ship. She caught herself in time; she stumbled up from her pallet and out into the cabin while the ship groaned and pitched around her. She could hear the muffled high winds through the walls of the vessel and staggered up the stairs. Wind tore at her clothing. Rain drove into her face, but she preferred it to the stifling room below decks. She clung to the bannister at the top of the stairs as the vessel pitched and yawed. Sailors were taking down the sails. Others were securing ropes and pulling winches. The helmsman fought the great steering wheel midships as a huge wave crashed across her side of the boat, sending a slash of spume and dark water across the decks. The vessel rolled and Fela caught herself. The captain saw her and boomed, "Get below decks!"

Fela ignored him. She felt the ferocity of the sea, its rampant wildness, and she was rooted to the spot. The winds tore at her and whipped white froth from the tops of the waves. The ship plowed into another trough, and the captain turned away. A shout came from one of the sailors.

"Eyes! Eyes in the water!"

"Yer mad!"

"No! There! And there!"

The captain shouted above the roar of the wind. "Get to your work and keep your hands steady!"

The oars of the vessel were out and she watched as they tried to find purchase in the heaving seas and then she saw them. An onyx glow of eyes in the cresting of a wave. And then they blinked out as the foam burst and flew. There were at least 10 pairs of eyes, all gleaming darkly by the light of the lanterns that hung over the wheel. The Ota sang joyously in Fela's mind. They are here, they are here!

The sailors were gathering along the port side as the ship went over and into another trough and wallowed out, taking a great wash of wave across the bowsprit.

"It's ocean devils! The ship is doomed! They're luring us to the rocks!" There was yelling and the captain began shouting in a rage. "Get back to your posts! It's naught but a school of squid! Ye white bellied crab bait!"

As the boat came up out of the trough, she saw them again in a thundering wave that caught the ship on its side. The eyes watched; they rolled again under the waves. The men went wild; many of them left their stations and were gesticulating at the waves, looking around with fear in their eyes, and several turned to point at her. "It's the witch! She's called sea monsters! The evil that sleeps in the deep! She's called them up!" The men gathered along the port side and many of them were now rounding on her. Suddenly the captain strode for Fela and grabbed her arm hard. "You're a bad one. A witch, a Nameless godless terror! I should've never allowed you on the ship! Moldock, Pith! Lower the skiff! Get this creature off!"

She was hauled roughly by both arms towards the tiny lifeboat. She slipped in the rain and wind and one of the men caught her, picked her up bodily, and tossed her into the craft. She heard the winches lowering the boat. The captain threw in a keg of water as an afterthought.

"Good riddance! I'll not have my men in a terror over your witchery, woman!" They let go the ropes and Fela's little boat caught the cresting waters.

The Ota in her soaked pocket sang sweetly. It is well, it is well! Fela, her heart pounding, fumbled to find the oars, as a huge wave threatened to roll her over; she managed to dip the oars down but they were heavy, and the wind blew the boat around.

Fela rode cresting wave after cresting wave and several times, she saw the eyes again. She regained her courage and fought with the sea, watching the ship disappear in the huge swells.

She rowed until the strength went from her to keep the craft righted, she rowed until her back ached and she was chilled through to the bones. But she would not give up. She didn't know how long she rowed. The storm, over time, began to blow itself out. The waters grew calmer. The rain abated. The eyes disappeared and Fela, adrift in the dark, curled up with the singing Ota and fell into a witless, black sleep of despair.

CHAPTER NINE

The Island of the Seals

Fela was being gently rocked from side to side by her mother. Her mother was singing a tuneless song in her low voice and Fela curled deeper into her lap. She was safe, safe and home and her mother was warming her. She never had to leave her mother. She could stay here forever.

She opened her eyes as the dream faded. The world shifted and righted itself; she was in a small craft now beached on gravel. As each wave struck the shore, the boat rocked again. The cold covered her like a heavy dank blanket.

She felt in her pocket and there was the Ota, asleep and still warm. Fela relaxed a little.

The beach was narrow, and not welcoming. Drifting fog wisped like a curtain, obscuring everything.

Where was she? How far had she travelled in the night, during the storm?

She stood up, shaking, and hauled the boat out as far as she could across the beach, thanking Tun and the Moon Twins and every lesser goddess and god her mother had taught her about for her life and safety.

She collapsed onto the sand and pebbles. The rocks were slick and slimy with sea life. Wine colored seaweed and white whorled shells covered some of the boulders. She got the jug of water out and drank deeply. The pouch she carried was still around her shoulder. She took out the last of the jerky.

She was alive. She had survived that devil of a captain and his cowardly crew. She had touched each of them. She knew they quailed from life's cruelty and were terrified of shadows. Her mother...she heard her mother's warning words with new ears. Her mother had been right. Something hardened inside her. If folk were witless and ignorant, if their terror could lead them to toss innocent people to their sure deaths...she would have to disguise herself. But her anger at the injustice flared over her life, bright with sudden clarity. It showed clearly the love of her father, who wanted her to know who and what she was. He wanted her to know the depths of her power. He had put himself in harm's way to help her.

And what had he said? About the three jewels of the Enduil? His last wish to her was to find them, and restore the balance of the world. She laughed out loud. She was sure she would die here, but not this very moment. She had a little water, a little food; she wasn't dead yet.

She explored the craft and found a packet of tools lashed to the stern...a coil of twine, a flint, a small knife, some steel rods, a strange stone. She took it all, then tied the boat to a driftwood log, above the tide line.

She could see that animals...deer or riverine otter...had

created a path up the steep curving side of the cove.

She made her way up it to the top of the ridge, carrying the jug of water.

By the time she reached the top, the winds had blown away most of the fog. She thought she might be on an island.

The top of this bluff was mostly meadow. Brown grasses and straggling wild rose, winter-burnt, grew sparsely on the rocky ground. Through the mist she could make out a distant tree line. She would need a place out of the wind to shelter, and she made her way to them.

The light barely changed as she crossed the wide meadow. She reached the trees and walked over hills, climbing over decaying logs, pushing through harsh berry vines until she reached the other side—it was an island— where she found a hollow between three gnarled juniper trees, so contorted by the wind that their twisted limbs looked like spectres.

She could hear the breakers below. On the edge of the trees again, she watched an eagle dive and dive again, fighting with a gull. At the edge of the cliff she looked down on a beach, more welcoming than the one she'd landed on. It was curved like the horn of a moon. She decided to call it moon beach.

A movement caught her eye. An otter, she thought, digging in the sand. It dug and scraped, and out popped a dark circular object. Fela clambered down to the beach and began to dig herself, watching the otter hump away from her with its treasure. She had heard her father talk of clams and oysters.

She found a stick to dig with, and dug as the tide came in. Eventually she had six clams to show for her hard work.

Water trickled out of a seam in the rock. She tasted it. It

was fresh! She filled her jug. She sat on the dry sand and rested. The air was warmer now, but still damp and heavy. She squinted into the half-light. Up on the ridge the dark trees stood like watchful sentries. She stood on trembling legs and went back to prod the sand for tell-tale clam squirts when she saw movement at the other end of the beach. She stilled, barely breathing.

It was a man. No, a youth. He had been behind a large boulder that sat upon the shore and now he was making his way towards her. He stopped. Fela's heart was pounding. She watched him lean against a large rock to support himself. Was he hurt? Had he been shipwrecked too?

Her heart was now going like a frightened hare's. Did he need food as well? They had always shared, in her home. Her mother, baking cakes, her hands working over millet and apples, and coarse salt...she closed her eyes. She would not think of her mother, but she knew what it was to be hungry. But she had barely gathered enough for herself. And he could also be dangerous.

The boy stared at her, barely able to walk. He grabbed the boulder and could hardly keep his feet. Fela was transfixed. She made a decision.

The wind surrounded her with the scent of the rich sea as she made her way over the smooth pebbles of the beach. He watched her. She offered the clams as she walked, but suddenly he pulled himself up, tall and still as a heron, then made for the water and dove in.

She watched the ocean close over his head in a smooth black caress. Those waters were so very cold...no one could survive that for long.

She sat down on the beach and scanned the dark surface for some sign of the boy, but he was gone. Her hands began to shake. The rough outlines of the clams blurred in front of her eyes.

As soon as her sight cleared, she chose a rock, and smashed the clams. The flesh was wet, rubbery and gritty, but she wolfed them all, then curled in the damp sand and fell asleep.

When she awoke it was dusk. She felt a little better. She walked back to her camp inside the tough junipers, scraped together a bed of moss and bracken. After many minutes, she succeeded in starting a very small fire and feverishly, carefully, she built up the flames until she was sure embers would be left in the morning. Something inside of her untightened. If she could successfully start a fire, and push the night back, warm her body just a little, then she had a chance. A chance to survive. Night settled around her and she curled tight against it, huddled near the fire, then slept and dreamed.

In the dream she was walking through her village. The Ota had invited her to visit, and this felt like the most natural thing in the world. Fela arrived. The Ota's home was built into a hill, the door was polished horn and Fela called, and the door opened slowly and she went in. Ota was there, a beautiful young woman, short and comely with almond shaped eyes and silvery hair that flowed over and around her shoulders like water. They ate fruit from a plate and the Ota said, Afelanua. I have wondrous gifts for you. One is invisible, and lives in the heart. The other is a gift returned. It's deeper in the house. Wait, and I will find it." Fela waited, and wandered from one room to the next. There was a picture of a handsome youth in one of the rooms, and many strange implements in others, and she woke shivering in the cold gray dawn.

Her hand reflexively went to where the Ota slept and she

was gone. Fela searched around the stones, she brushed through the pine needles, she pushed her wood pile aside, but she could not find the Ota.

Trying to calm herself, she cleared her mind and called, then waited, eyes closed, in the morning chill.

Softly, softly she felt a gentle, very slight pressure. All is well. Home. Home! And gifts! Gifts for you! Then…nothing. Fela beseeched and waited, and begged for the Ota's voice over and over again, but all was silence.

Now, even the Ota was gone.

After a while, she gathered herself up and steeled her mind. She needed food. The sky was clear this morning. She decided to climb to a barren peak she could see, to look over the island for better places to find clams.

She found a deer path through the thorns and brush. The high outcropping didn't look that far away, but she had learned that distance was deceptive. The air was cold, but the sun shone like a solid shield of light. Towards mid-morning she reached the base of the stone outcropping, and began her ascent with care, leaning on her digging stick as she made her way up the steep ridges and boulders. She routed herself closer to the sea as she climbed, and paused now and then to catch her breath. Seals darted below in the sea, or lounged on their bellies, drying their flippers. They looked like bloated wineskins in the sun. The sight calmed her and she set her hand down on the rock for purchase, and in a trice was sent reeling back from the surge of magic she felt beneath her palm. It smacked like a tingling whip and left her breathless and her flesh quivering in excitement. She stood still for minutes under the sun. Hope flooded her. The magic felt like a beacon, left purposefully.

She put down her stick and her jug, and balanced herself.

She felt with her palm back up to the strongest spot. The rock here fairly buzzed with lines of magic, like invisible golden ropes.

For most of the day she followed the rope. The strongest line was not much wider than her hand, but she could feel a low buzz at a distance, in both directions.

She followed it over the peak and down the far shoulders of stone that swept back into the island but at the edge of the rock the signal ran out.

In consternation, Fela followed it back again to the sea. The closer she got to the precipice, the stronger it became. With growing anxiety, she realized that the rope left to her by mages long gone disappeared over the shadowy overhang of rock and into the boiling sea.

She left the invisible rope and clambered down and around. She walked along the edge of the overhang, across boulders covered with rough lichens and gull droppings, and finally stopped and looked back from whence she had come. There. She could see it now; a dark opening below the invisible rope. There was no beach below, only foaming ocean and a sharp cut of the cove.

She fretted. To jump into such a sea, that stirred and roiled from the collision of tide with rock, would be certain death. She climbed up and away from the hard edge of the island and walked slowly back toward her shelter. The sun had set and the wind was picking up. In her excitement she had forgotten about her hunger.

She closed her eyes and opened them again. A figure darted out over the rocks below...it looked like the youth who had leapt to his death into the water! Her scalp prickled...did he live here as well? How had he survived the freezing waters? She steadied herself, trying to slow her fast heart. She must have food. But night was coming on.

She scrabbled on the slippery stones and began the climb down over tumbled rock and the tough roots of trees. Flashing lights danced in front of her eyes and she rested to catch her breath. It was useless. The beach would be too dark by the time she arrived. She turned and started climbing back to camp again.

Something tugged on the inside of her eyelids and forced her to wakefulness. The moon was bright and full above her and light sluiced down through the juniper boughs and shone on her nest of cedar needles and deer moss. She sat up. Spread out in front of her cold fire pit was a shining fish, and a mound of clams, cracked open. She listened, the hairs on the back of her neck prickling. All she heard was the soughing of wind through cedar and juniper. All she saw was the strange silver light of the moon lancing through the dark. But far away, down the sloping meadow, she thought she heard an animal rushing through the dead grasses. She sat for a long time listening, and then she ate the clams, and built a bigger fire for the fish, and ate half the fish.

That night, as Fela lay curled in her bed of moss, she returned to the memory of the tingling whip of magic that she had found. She closed her eyes, and like the memory of the stone runes that had been carved into the cave walls, there came the shadow-feeling of another intent, another whisper of urgency behind the golden sizzle of the magic itself. She concentrated. She went through the memory. It was like teasing through the complex threading of rope; on the surface was the first sensation and the strongest: magic itself. But if she let the memory relax in her mind, there was, beneath that, a dark shadow. And beneath the strands...she let out breath. A hand, trembling. Hunger. Loneliness. She began to catch the shadows' shapes within the snaking threads... shipwrecked, abandoned, a broken leg, a family missed, heartbreak at a mission not accomplished. She kept teasing through the shadows. There was a smell of rotten fish, the bright light of a clear sunlit day, a bleeding thumb. And then...as she pressed further, a memory of two people, in robes of rich saffron, who pressed their hands on his head and the vision unfurled so quickly and suddenly, surprising her...that it was hard to grasp it all. She was standing in a hall made of cut stone and two enduil were smiling at her. There were many blazing sconces, a sweet scent like honey or spice, and the sounds of music resonating in the background. They placed the instrument in her hands, some kind of ceremony...a shell, fashioned like a conch or a triton. It shone gleaming ebony in the bright light; the protuberant spines upon it like a diminishing frill of lace. He...for Fela was now seeing the man as the man who had left the trail of magic...was known by the two enduil, respected, and abashed because of the great honor being bestowed upon his family and him. He was to take this Black Triton from the Empire of At and present it as an act of fealty to the Black Prince, a gesture that was hoped would cement an alliance between the Attish Empire, and the hitherto enemy of the Tundin and the Northern Palinisar. The gesture wasn't an empty gesture; this was a last hope to cement the country's powers in order to stop Finauld, who was terrorizing the land. His name was Geland, and his entourage, en route overseas to the mainland, had been waylaid by pirates. In an act of sabotage, Geland had been shipwrecked with nothing but the Black Triton, and now sick, starving, he had only his powers as a mage and a need, which Fela felt clearly, to hide the Triton. Geland had escaped. But not a seaman, and at the mercy of a late squall, he had ended up here on the island. His desire to hide the Triton from the enemy who still sought him and the Black Triton, above all, drove him.

Fela received this vision in a flash of hope that sparked like gunpowder through the tactile information she sifted through. But then, just as quickly...the memory flared out, and there was nothing more. Fela kept her eyes closed and sought for more from the memories she had, but there was nothing left. Her eyes were open wide in the darkness. The Black Triton! Here, somewhere, on the island! And had Geland had help? Had he left that mark on the rocks to guide someone like herself? But how in Tun was she to reach that treacherous point below the crashing surf, where the mark of magic so clearly pointed? She lay back, staring up into the dark forms of the swaying pines overhead. How could this be, that, shipwrecked herself, she had floundered onto the same island in which her father and her Uncle Pib were interested? She would have laughed if she had had the energy.

She sighed, and reached over to build up her own fire. She would go back in the morning to see if there was more to be had, more to be sifted through, from the invisible trail of magic left on the rocks and to think about finding a way down. It seemed unbelievable that such an object would be on this strange rock in the middle of the ocean. Was this why the Ota had been so joyous? She watched the fire, thinking, and soon fell back into a more settled sleep.

CHAPTER TEN

The Trail of Magic

That night she dreamed of the monster. They were in the bedroom, where the woman had been raped. Agadittur was standing beside the bed, a small closed smile on his face. "Don't you wonder where your father is, Afelanua? Don't you want to know? I can take you to him. Come. Come with me." Compelled by some dream-insistence, Fela could not disobey. And then they were flying, flying through the night air, and Agadittur was a dragon and she had changed as well but she was bound to him in some way; she could not escape his presence. They flew over mountain ranges with the cold dead stars burning in the night sky above. They landed near the great curve of a river in the woods.

The smell assaulted her before they came up on two shacks. Mixed in with the stench of offal and piss was the scent of a large animal that was freshly dead. Dark huts built of logs and thatch mouldered by the side of the path and as Agadittur took her through the squalid mire Fela heard the soft rustle of wings and ice-cold horror flooded her skin. In the dark, across from the huts, she saw a dozen black vultures rise, disturbed from their carnage. They rose up into the trees like a black fog and as Fela's eyes followed their flight up, there, in a single torchlight's fumy shadows, hung a body tied to a post. Strung up by the arms, the head hung at a grotesque angle onto the chest and the skin had been flogged from even the front of the dead man's thin ribs. But Fela knew the shape of the torso, the angle of the stubborn chin, the black hair on the forearms.

"I'll find you, Nameless bitch. I found your father and in the end, I'll find you, as well." Fela woke from the horror with the sound of Agadittur's soft laughter still in her ears. She sat up. The sun was high and bright and the wind had died down.

She stuffed dry deer moss into the smoking crevice of the log and added more twigs, but her hands shook and would not leave off shaking. Something niggled in the back of her mind as she tried not to think of her father, whipped and dead, in the nightmare. The dreamscape had been so real, Agadittur's laugh and the stench of death overpowering. Despair tore at her like a faceless black animal. She had to turn her mind to something concrete, something she could do to rid herself of the horror of her father's dream-death. And the boy? Had he brought the food? She still had some fish. She had hard work ahead of her and she forcibly turned her thoughts to the lines of magic that had disappeared down into the churning sea. How was she to get to that cove below the ledge of stone, where the mark ended?

Her skin shrank from the bright cold of the day. She had to hurry. She put more wood on, and the smell of cedar reminded her of her mother, weaving baskets. Her mother used to say that the Tundin once made their clothing out of cedar bark. And not only clothing, she said. Weapons, baskets, rope, clothing, blankets....red cedar protected the Tundin for centuries. She said it was only later that the Green Lady had brought weaving and the use of wool to the people.

Fela remembered watching her father strip a section of a cedar tree. He took the strips and quickly made it into good strong rope, strong enough to use in breaking colts. Fela thought. The next low tide was later in the day, and the next low tide after that was, after she slept, in mid-morning. She could try to weave a rope and then, at low tide, try to lower herself into the cavern, but she had to hurry.

As the fire popped and took, she cut the boy's offering with the little knife, skewered and cooked it, and ate the rest of the fish, but she could not rid her mind of the sight of her father's broken and torn body.

When she had eaten, she looked through the forest until she found an old red cedar. The boat's little knife stood her in good stead, but it took her much longer than she'd thought. Sweat dampened her ratty tunic and her fingers were full of whiskery splinters by the time she carried her bundle of bark strips along the path toward her camp in the trees.

Along the way, she put down her bundle and left the deer path to walk out on the cliff again. She needed to guess at the length of rope she would need. She emerged from the trees in time to see the sun setting like a red disc on the horizon. She had just enough time to make it to the base of the stone mountain.

A cold wind tightened her skin as she walked back along

the cliff. When she looked down at the distance to the cave below, her stomach sank. The amount of rope she would need would take her almost all of the next day to make, unless she started tonight and kept at it. Her hands were already raw, and she was bone-cold with hunger.

Below, the seals met her gaze. They regarded her in silence, their dark eyes reminding her of the boy's alien stare. She pulled her ripped cloak to her thin flesh and left the darkening air and the biting wind for her shelter. At least there would be fire, if not food, there.

That night the wind tore through the tops of the junipers in gusts so long and fierce that boughs snapped and crashed around her to the forest floor. Her fire, even in the lee of her bowl-like shelter, guttered low and flattened itself to the firepit floor. In between the raging blasts of wind she piled on more wood and tried to warm herself. Her center shook and shivered so that she could not hold her frozen hands still as she worked. The rough bark plunged splinters into every chapped crack in her hands, but she kept on long after the cold sun set.

She worked, twisting and braiding the strips of bark, then tying the lengths together. She tested her knot's strength and went onto the next. The winds howled around her, low and fearsome. Shadows moved. The work kept her mind from the well of fear in her pinched belly. She built up the fire, which bloomed one minute and was squashed the next by the harsh palm of the wind.

She was determined not to stop until exhaustion blinded her or she ran out of rough strips. It was very late. The moon hung bright and the wind wracked the treetops and there came a horrendous shriek that rolled through the night. Fela's hands stopped dead.

Her soul filled with panic. The monster had found

her....as the dark thing tore through the branches, Fela dropped the cedar strips and groped blindly for the knife, hidden beneath her bedding. The monster plunged toward her and fear squeezed her chest so tightly that her lungs fought to draw air. The branch crashed down beside her firepit and showered her with rotting bark and pine needles.

She dropped the knife and her weeping erupted out of her numb center in a torrent she could not stop. Her hands shook and long strands of snot hung from her cold nose and she wept until the moon crept down from its high place.

She woke in the morning to stillness. Her cheeks and chin were crusted with mucus and dried tears, but most of the cedar rope lay in a neat coil at the foot of her bed. She sat up. The sky was gray and there was no sign of Agadittur and his evil that she feared. It had just been a branch, brought down by the wind. The threat of rain hung in the cold air. She sighed and rolled over and wished for the scented fat that her mother used to soothe chapped skin. But there was none of that, nor was there food. She knew she would have to find sustenance today, or she would not have the strength to face the black precipice down into the hidden cave. But she was so close to finishing the rope! She placed more wood on the glowing embers, retrieved her satchel and stick, and set back out to strip bark from the cedar tree. Later, she promised herself, she would hunt clams on moon beach. She had to finish the rope. She was so close.

She spent most of the day finishing the rope by the cedar tree. Finally she headed back to her camp to drop the rope before heading to Moon Beach. She found the deer path that led back to her shelter. She sidled through the primroses, and pushed through boughs, stooping and standing at last beside her firepit.

There was something else there that had not been there before she left. She stopped. She listened as early evening and the birds around her settled in the dusk, but all she heard was the wind singing through the juniper and cedar, and all she saw were the dark shapes of stone and tree, stone and tree tiering up and away into the dark heart of the island beyond, with the golden light of sunset turning the limbs of the trees into lines of radiance. She moved closer. She could see another fish, and a mound of opened mussels. But the youth, for she knew it was the youth bringing her the sea's wealth, was not to be seen.

She set about making a fire with the precious stone and shortly had weak flames started from deer moss and sappy twigs. She eyed the fish. She was very hungry and the deep relief at not having to hunt for food in the dusky evening made her anxiety lessen. But something that her father had said once about gifts given needing another gift flashed again through her tired mind, the recollection odd and troubling. She gathered as many dry branches and limbs as she could find, and brought them back to the fire.

Something made her glance up. In the firelight across from her, under a tall cedar, hunkered the youth.

This close to her, his silent physicality was very frightening. She set the branches down. She watched his eyes and tried to slow her heartbeat. His eyes were dark as coals, and they glowed with anger, and some other need for which she had no language. She could see that a wound on his arm had knit closed, though it was still swollen and red. His skin was very dark, olive-brown, and shone glistening in the firelight. He wore no covering or cloak. His genitals were only half-hidden by glossy black hair that covered his lower belly like the pelt of an animal, and his hands hung over the tops of his bent knees. His feet…but that could not be right.

She looked back at his hands, and his face. She watched him swallow. He was thin, but ropy with muscle, his hands and feet too big still for his body. She realized he was still a boy in much the same way that she was still a girl. It embarrassed her but made her feel more at home with him. He motioned to the mussels. He made a noise in his throat, and motioned again. He made the noise again, and this time she realized he was saying "eat." He spoke the common speech, like her, but it was some odd dialect she had never heard before.

"Thank you." Her voice sounded odd. She had been silent so long.

"Eat." He watched her. "You work hard. In the wind so long. No food." He stared at her. He looked around her shelter, and his eyes came back to her body.

"How….how did your arm…"

"Spider moss. On land. My dam fetched for me and it helped." She saw him tense to stand up but his eyes waited for her to direct him.

"No, I mean…never mind. You can come closer to the fire."

He stood up with the litheness of an animal and came and sat down by the fire, across from her. He did not lose the wariness with which he held himself. Now she could see that his skin seemed almost oily under the light. His dark brown hair was long and ran in a svelte curtain down his back, as svelte as the pelt at his lower belly. She looked away from him. He was beautiful in a very wild way, the way wind is beautiful or the angry sea.

"Where is your herd? Your male?" He picked up one of the mussels and handed it to her.

She took it but she paused before she brought its flesh to her mouth. "I was left here, by bad people. And I've found a sign, left long ago, that might lead me to something good. For something that...might have been lost by my people. We... we have a storm coming, a bad storm, and this thing might be able to help us live through the storm. That's what my father told me."

"But no one to protect you?" His eyes were very dark and his mouth seemed set. She looked directly into his eyes, and saw so much sorrow entwined with the anger there that she had to look away. Without thinking she ate the shellfish. He handed her another. They ate them all, one at a time, not speaking further. She wiped her hands on the lichen-covered stone behind her. When she turned around he was so close his scent filled her senses. Some strong sea musk, and a sweet scent that made her belly twist in a surprise of arousal, and a stronger smell, like the lather of working horses. He pressed her back and down into her bed nest and she tried to push him off with all of her strength. He bit into the side of her neck and his hands tore at her tattered cloak. She twisted out from underneath him in a furious spasm and put her hand against his throat and he paused. His eyes were terrible, and stunned with need.

She was breathing very hard. "Stop! Stop...."

"But...you have no male! You took my food!"

Her heart crashed in her chest. She was very frightened. She watched him and his own breathing was harsh and she saw his hungry eyes fill with tears. His breath hissed through clenched teeth. "You took my food! Why do you stop me?" Before they could exchange words or anger he stood up in a crouch and ran, ran back into the wall of scratching primroses and the windy blanket of night. And just like that, he was gone. She had wanted to ask him how he had been wounded. She had wanted to ask him about the cove below the stone mountain. But all she was left with was the memory of his dark eyes and the pressure of his body.

She wrapped the fish in leaves and kept it close by. She did not sleep for a long time that night.

As she roused to morning, she remembered the youth, and the hunger in his eyes, and knew now what he had wanted. She sat up and found the fish. She took her fire stick and prodded the fire to see if there were embers from last night, and found a wisping curl of smoke under a large piece of wood. He could have forced himself on her, but he had not. He could have overpowered her and done what he wished, but instead he had fled into the night. He brought her food, but when she broke the rule of his gift, which was not her rule, he left her alone. She ate the fish sparingly, for she knew there would be no more. She hefted her coil of rope, and went to seek out the cove below the stones.

CHAPTER ELEVEN

Strange Gifts

She made for the hills, climbed across their ponderous forms, and looked down into the tumbling sea. Her stomach tightened in fear but she knew the rope was well made. She secured one end to a sturdy young pine growing in a crevice of the rock, and tied the other end around her waist.

Fela was slight, and strong, and could move quick as a darting bird. The day was calm and the light dull white, like the inside of an oyster's shell, and not as cold as yesterday, but she shivered, from excitement, from fear, as she made her way haltingly down that great curving stone face that sloped into the sea below, keeping the rope tight and testing, testing all the way. Crouched mid-way down, still with her feet grasping and secure, she looked down at the frothing ocean and her heart lightened. The tide was going out and revealed a small sliver of beach beneath the daunting stone ledge. Hand over hand, she let herself down, and made sure, once again, that she had rope enough left for her to heave herself up to the stone face. She feared she lacked the strength but she knew if her arms gave out that the sea would bear her weight, and float her up to the rock cliff. She hoped it did not come to that.

Fela dropped down lightly onto the rock-strewn sand below her and slid in the wet shur of the new beach. She trembled from excitement and ran her hands over the underside of the stone wall that receded into darkness. There! The sign of magic sparked and tingled under her hand! She peered into the narrow black shaft of the cavern before her and ducked. Only a little light made its way into the cleft. She bent over and walked in. It was close and cold and the rank salt scent of the ocean overwhelmed her...the rot of ages and a rich mineral scent with putrefaction of flesh and the salty tang of ocean combined to overwhelm her senses. An odd pinkish light lit the rocks and the movement of the tide pool made the shadows ripple and dance against the steep rock sides. She took off her battered boots and left them outside. She stepped into cold seawater and moved as far forward as she could but though the cave widened, it deepened as well and she could see before her that the cavern also sloped down, down into the belly of the island, below the great stones that made the bedrock of this place. It was filled with the sea, though a small bridge of sand remained between the beach she had come from and the narrow way into the cave. A sea she could not surmount, deep and unreachable. Now the full weight of her despair came and sat solid on her shoulders. The Ota had left her; the strange boy who brought food had asked silently for a payment she was not prepared to give. She was tantalized with clues to a strange treasure, and she had no means forward, an impossible obstacle in her way.

She had come so far! Fretting, angry, she left the cave and hunted all up and down the tiny strip of exposed beach, but already waves were again lapping close around her feet. The tide was licking hungrily at the rocky coast and she explored quickly to the right side of the cave as well. There was, she could see, a small strip of sand and rock that went around a promontory but from this angle she could not see what lay past that rocky point. Now the tide was pooling around her feet; she'd need all her energy to hoist herself back up the stone face, but she wanted to explore around that high sloping edge.

She tried, but it was too perilous; the rocks were slick and if she lost her footing she could hurt herself grievously. Defeated for the moment, Fela grabbed her rope and after several breathless moments, she clambered and scrambled, pulled and hoisted herself, and at the fourth attempt, she found her footing on the rock face. Carefully, meticulously, she made her way gripping with her feet and her hands so tight her arms began to tremble. At last she made the sturdy little tree and undid her stout rope. Distantly, she heard thrashing, and thought not much of it but desiring to see what lay behind that promontory from above, she made her way along the steep ridgeline, and looked down. There was a small cove below her, and a very steep otter path down, but what made her catch her breath were two seals in the cove, slashing and fighting. One was large, black, and glistened with muscular strength as its tusks flashed in the afternoon light. The other seal, longer and more sinuous, twisted and ducked the bigger seal's attacks. And in a great leap of understanding, she knew one of the seals was the boy. She sought the path down, but it was very steep, very treacherous, and by the time she got down to the driftwood-littered cove, the youth was heaving himself from the sea, no longer in seal form. Black blood streamed from a wound on the inside of his thigh, so ragged and long she knew he would die from blood loss if nothing were done to staunch the wound. She ran, picking her way over the mounds of driftwood, down to the rocky beach. She helped him drag himself ashore. She looked around frantically.

"Dogwort," he gasped. "There." He pointed, gasping. "Seedpods." She hurried to the cove's corner where straggling brown plants stood in a stand and she gathered the seedpods, which were filled with a cottony fluff. She filled her tunic and laid them up on the beach. She looked around. The driftwood made a kind of shelter if she moved one or two scattered pieces. She saw another freshet of water seeping down the steep cliff wall of this cove and she helped half-drag the youth as he lost his footing into the protection of the driftwood. He lay finally still, and turned his face away from her. She pulled the stuff from the seedpods and made a poultice of them and though she knew it was terrible, she began stuffing the gaping wound with the fibers. His hands clenched the sand and his jaw spasmed hard. Fela collected water in her hands and washed the edges of the wound, going again and again to the freshet, finally using a broad leaf she found that had floated into the cove. The boy was shivering, but she had no cloth with which to cover him. The light was short in these late winter days and Fela had her flint with her. Painstakingly, she started a fire from bracken and dried driftwood and built it up against the back of an old huge log. The youth, unconscious or asleep, moved no more, and Fela stayed awake and watched the red sun lower in the sky until it went to dull red ash, then gray, then black. Her little fire kept her busy the night long as she strove to feed it with damp wood that smoked and fretted. The boy slept, but it was not an easy sleep, and Fela, leaning against the great log by the fire, succumbed to sleep as well.

Acrid smoke peeled Amemne out of dreams of rippling moonlight and churning black water; he fought up and out of the nightmare with the hot tusk still impaled in his leg and the huge dark male crushing him to the ocean floor. He couldn't breathe, he couldn't breathe. A hand shook him out of the swaying kelp and the weight of the giant male and he came to, with the smoke burning his eyes and his leg throbbing like a drum. He humped his back upwards to escape but the hand on him, with the fingers points of pressure on his shoulder, pressed him down. A voice hummed in his head, pitched low. He dropped his head back into the sand and saw the white of the moon overhead, hanging like a round stone in the milky swirl of stars.

The pain in his leg was huge; it was like a wide-open mouth caught in a scream that went on, and on. The voice in his ears spoke words and he tried to see who it was. He moved his head and he saw that he was in a cave of driftwood; a small fire sizzled at their feet. The form, small and dark, but human, the girl! The girl who had denied him! She was pushing a cold poultice of kelp into the long sluice of his opened thigh. The cool felt good for just a moment and then a huge red flower of pain cracked his skull and he convulsed. Shame and anger armed him to the teeth and he vomited up a rivulet of sour water. He could not bear the shame. He heaved himself over, mindless of his wound. The poultice slopped off and he scrabbled wildly at the driftwood. His nails caught on soft ocean-drenched splinters and did nothing. His mind was full of Bullkelp looming, the huge male's bubbles surrounding him in a spray of gassy evil, and being pressed down, and down and to his utter horror, the larger male had forced him on his side before he had sliced Amemne through, like he was not even a rival male but a female. His brain ran in circles trying to find a way out of that conclusion and he could find none. In the recollection of this shame and the shame of receiving help from the girl, Amemne writhed on the sand and tore furiously at the driftwood, pushing at the shelter. He ignored the soft hands that fluttered over him like the breath of the young female for which he had fought. The hands tightened on him and he was too weak to go further. He lay with his mouth open in the sand. He closed his eyes and tried to stop the hissing of his hot breath through his teeth.

The youth's limbs flailed in the moonlight. Fela tried to calm him with her hands, and with her voice, but he seemed delirious and the fever added fuel to the fire of his distress. She was already exhausted. There had not been enough food again that day. She had spent too long on the stones, in the drying wind and under the brass gong of the sun, running her hands over the hard fissures of rock and over the succulents growing in the cracks, exploring the cavern, fretting and searching for that tingle of magic that could lead her home, that might provide an answer to her father's riddle. And then, the attack, the youth who had helped her. The young man had finally fallen off into a dead sleep. But he had struggled so and for so long, that she had begun to despair. She had leaned against the nest of driftwood and waited for his hoarse cries to rattle off.

Now, she nudged dry shards of driftwood onto the ruby embers. She pressed the poultice back into the wound, and minded to fetch fresh kelp in the morning to change out the dressing. She dribbled fresh water from a clamshell onto his cracked lips and curled up against him for warmth as the night was cold and he was shaking from the attack. And she wondered if she would find what was right beneath her nose, or if she would starve first. The wind soughed through the tortured trunks of the junipers up on the ridge above, and Fela pulled her robe across her chest, pulled her knees up against the shaking torso of the boy, and locked herself away from her hungry flesh. Morning would come.

She woke. The wind was spitting cold rain into her face. The fire at her feet was dead and black. The boy was gone. Driftwood from her makeshift shelter was scattered where he had kicked out a hole to make his escape.

She looked at the horizon. The sky was blank gray. Just the cold rain and wet stones of the beach. There was no sign of the youth. She had seen the anger in his eyes, felt his anger even in the depth of his delirium. What had happened to him? The awful carving in his thigh…she had tried to staunch the bleeding and thought that she had, but he wouldn't live long unless he minded his wound. Her eyes swept the rocks and niches of the cove walls, and out beyond, to the finger of stone that jutted in front of the cove far off. No dark shape of the boy, no movement. Gone.

She got up, her body tired from the night and stiff from her adventure in the cave yesterday. She took her digging stick and satchel and went back to Moon Beach to dig the elusive clams there. She had to have food.

She spent the day on her hands and knees, waiting and watching for the little telltale squirts, and by sundown she had eaten enough to fill her belly. She was making for her camp when some inner knowing turned her. She went back to Seal Cove, where she had found him so direly wounded. In the dying light of day she made her way down the treacherous narrow path to the beach below and she stopped. The youth lay on his side, shivering, inside of the driftwood shelter. The satchel of remaining clams banging against her leg, she hurried down to the boy.

Throughout the night, she tended the fire and tried to bring his fever down. Delirious, he arched off of the sand and screamed hoarsely at an unseen foe. She tried to soothe him with her hands, she tried to get him to lie still but he batted her hands away and flashed his teeth at her, his eyes rolling. She brought him water, over and over again in larger clam shells, trying not to trip over the driftwood logs in the night. She changed out the cooling kelp poultice in the inflamed gash of his leg and thought his death was very near. In the dark heart of the night, so still and cold that frost formed on driftwood around her, as she carefully nursed the scant fire, he seemed to sleep deeply. Not the fitful sleep of a fever-harassed mind, but a true sleep.

Fela slept herself, then, and didn't wake until the morning crept in over the sea and opened up into a mist-cloaked dawn. The youth was once again gone. This time, there was no sign of his leaving. She sighed. Sore and tired, she gathered herself, and headed back to her little shelter in the juniper trees.

CHAPTER TWELVE

The Wounded Boy

She pressed through the low branches and stepped into her camp under the junipers, and saw the food. Two shining fish and a pile of clams, their shells gleaming mahogany. She could sense the youth, but couldn't see him. She began gathering deer moss and lichen from the stones to start her fire. She spoke into the oncoming night.

"You can come closer; I won't hurt you."

Motionless, he remained on the rock. He stared at her, his mouth drawn down. Unnerved, but calm, she continued gathering lichen. But her heart sang. Alive and well enough to hunt, to swim! She scratched and scratched again with the flint at the little pile of deer moss she used for fire starter. A spark smoked and flamed. She sheltered the tiny growing fire between her palms, trying to still her too-fast heart.

He stared at her, then watched the fire. "My

herd....everyone....tells me to stay away from you. But I have been run off, so it doesn't matter anymore."

"But why?" She was afraid even her glance would send him running through the woods and away over the meadow. But she stole one, anyway. His dark eyes shimmered with tears.

"Because I was weak." With this admission he stood up in a half crouch. "You can get the mussels from the cave, the cave on the east end." He turned to make for the junipers.

Fela shouted. "Wait!" There was a command to her voice and to her astonishment, he stopped.

He sat back down on his haunches and watched her. "Why are you here? Where is your herd? Isn't your mother worried for you?"

Her face stilled at that. "Will you share the shellfish?"

"Then you think me a coward, too." The sullen look was back. He retreated into his dark glower.

His brooding put her at ease, for it reminded her of her father in his bad moods and she laughed, and rocked back on her tailbone, legs crossed in front. "I think you're upset about what happened in your....herd." She moved a tendril of dark hair behind her ear. "I don't think you're a coward."

"Why not?" He stuck his chest out. Fela rejoiced. He hadn't shot off into the dark. "The women won't look at me any longer. The one I had...the one I wanted won't speak to me. She runs now. It's the way, but no one told me...no one told me how much it would spear me, inside." His eyes again filled with tears. He swiped at them.

She waited, and filled a nest of leaves with some of the shellfish. "You don't have to leave here. I don't have a mother, or a herd. I'm by myself." She offered the food. "Would you like some of the shellfish?"

He took it from her. His hand was smooth. "Did your herd….disown you? Is there something wrong with you?" He was instantly suspicious….he lowered his head to the ground and tipped forward. He closed his eyes and sniffed deeply around her work area near the fire. He looked just like one of the hounds her father used to keep. She smiled at that. He rose up and opened his eyes. "You're not sick. You're not pregnant. You smell normal, for a land-grub."

"A land-grub?" She stared at him.

He shrugged. "You can't breathe the proper water; you're of the land. White and soft and dry, like a grub." He smiled at her. His teeth were a strong, glistening white. He regarded her. "But you don't have a herd? No mother? Is this some sort of land magic?"

Fela frowned. She wrapped her arms tighter around her knees. "My mother died. She was murdered. My herd…I've found out that my herd…is scattered. I'm…I don't know how to describe this." She looked up at him. "Your people have magic, don't they? Strange sea magic?"

The young man nodded. "Yes. Wind, water, stone and shell. They all have the magic of the sea in them. You can cajole their magic, if you know the right songs, the right ways to please them." He flexed his toes. "It can be dangerous."

Fela looked off past the fire, out past the rocky point she could see through the juniper trees. She moved the same tendril again out of her face. "I have….a secret magic. It's very rare among my herd."

He sat down near the fire. It was chilly, but not cold. Even though he was naked, he didn't seem bothered by a lack of clothing; his pelt covered him in sensitive areas and his skin seemed thick and dark. He peered at her. "Your mother…was killed? By one of your own herd?"

"No. By another bad herd, a bad group of people, who want to use magic to destroy the world and make another world that they alone can control."

"Do you miss her?" His eyes remained mesmerized by her form.

Fela went silent. Suddenly she didn't want to eat. She stared down at the cooling mussels she had taken such pains to cook. She didn't want to think about her mother, or her father, her uncle…all the people she had left behind. She realized that the fire was the only thing keeping the dark and the silence and the roar of the ocean at bay; she was surrounded by hostile magic, a hostile, whipping sea, hostile seal-people who stared at her with their heads turned, one eye only watching, watching, from the surface of the waves. Her own eyes welled with tears.

"I have worried you. I have made you sad." He stood up, very angry. "Everywhere I go, I make more mistakes. I see my weakness. I wish I had not disturbed you."

"Wait….!" But he had gone. He didn't understand that it might have been better had he stayed.

She woke up suddenly in the middle of the night. He was sitting there; he had found more wood and the fire crackled and chuffed. It was cold and chill from the sea, but the fire threw warmth and friendly shadows. She sat up within her nest of pine needles. "You came back."

He, who had been staring at her ever since she had roused, now found other things to do with his eyes. "I saw that…you might have been sad. I was angry with myself, and couldn't see your sadness." He poked at the billowing fire with a stick. "Besides." He did look up at her again. "I want to know what happened to your mother; what kind of secret magic do you have that made you run from your herd?" He scooted closer to her nest. "Did you break a taboo? Did you refuse to mate with the leader? Did you hide a fine feeding grotto from the herd?"

'a fine feeding grotto'….Fela almost laughed, but did not, since the young man seemed so apt to run off. She stretched. Her eyes were crusty and she itched from the needles, though they were warm. "None of those things happened. I think now there was someone…and there might still be someone… after the kind of magic I can work."

"I knew. When I first saw you. You have what the sea has. The wildness of profound magic. Where you walk, the spirits make way."

Fela looked at the selkie boy, and there was silence between them. She could hear the wind making the tree boughs sing. "You could stay. You could stay on land, for a while." She didn't quite know what she was suggesting, but it seemed dangerous, a young man, vulnerable, angry, out by himself in the deep dark waters of a lonely ocean.

"You think I'm a coward. You think I'm not brave enough to go and establish my own herd. You're laughing at me, just like Seapeony did, when I was gored and bleeding…." His chest began to heave.

"No! No, I am not…" Before he could bolt, she was on her knees and had placed her hand on his arm. "I'm not laughing at all! I know what it's like to be alone! To be…different, set aside. Singled out." She relaxed slightly. One tear rolled down the young man's face. The pressure of her hand on his arm seemed to calm him instead of upsetting him, so she left it there. "Why are you so angry?" But she realized she knew the answer to that question….wounded viciously by a leader he had known since birth; cast out by the women who had raised him; goaded into challenging an older and much stronger opponent…he had many reasons to be angry. She realized it was a hopeless question.

But he answered anyway. "Because I've lost my home. I'll never see my mother comb her hair again in the morning, on the sandy beach. I'll never see Seapeony laugh again, dancing with the other girls. I won't hunt with Agate, or Seamonkey, or Urchin anymore, or hear the low horns blowing." He picked at a scab on his leg. "And…I am frightened. I'm angry because I'm very frightened. And it's shameful to not be brave." He closed his eyes and his breathing got more rapid.

"I think it's brave to admit that you're frightened."

"Why? You'll get pummeled for that."

She held out her hand to him. "No. If you know you're afraid, then you're on the road to figuring out what you're afraid of. Once you name the fear, then you can work on conquering it. Give me your hand."

He looked suspicious.

"I won't hurt you. It's my magic."

He put his hand in hers. Fela hung on tightly as the images flooded her mind. A huge, dark male's head was ravaging his leg….peals of a young woman's laughter….lost, lost in a hunting expedition….watching his father flee as a baby…and the ocean, seagrasses, a mother's warm close breath, tender hands, the lull of the tide, the wavering moonlight zigzagging silver through the black water…and the feral joy of the hunt, the dart through the cold clean water, the muscular arrowing zeal of hunting silver fish, the little white squid, all in a flashing school…she removed her hand.

"Your name is Amemne," she whispered. Her face flushed. He pulled him to her and nuzzled her cheek, and Fela let him. The fire burned down and all that night, they learned the ways of each other, what pleased, what made them laugh, and the joy that rests in the patience of love.

They whispered long into the night. Fela told him of her fruitless search, and how it had ended in the mouth of the great underwater cave. At this, Amemne became silent. He sat up, and stirred the fire.

"There were others, before you." He didn't look at her, but jabbed the coals of the fire with a stick. "They came in my dam's mother's time. My dam still has the small pretty things, some kind of shiny stone to wear in the hair, or the ears. I don't know." He glanced over his shoulder at Fela, who sat up on her elbows, listening. "They were gifts, these things. But my dam remembers this, because it has to do with the shama of the cave, the cave you say your signs have led you to."

Fela frowned. "What's shama?"

He leaned over and put more wood on the fire. "The ocean spirits' voice, or presence. Some spirits' voices are gentle and helpful. Others are…there. Maybe a warning. You are aware of that voice, but only as a presence, waiting." He turned fully to Fela. "It is an uncomfortable type of shama, but that type of feeling means no harm. Your cave, though… it is bad shama. The spirit who lives in this cave is old, older than stone, or the moon, or the ocean itself. It holds onto what it has been given." He turned back to the fire. "In my clans' memory, long ago, something was hidden there, something my people thought was dangerous, and they felt that bad belongs with bad, and so this object was hidden away in darkness, and given to the spirit who lives, deep and undisturbed, beneath this island."

Fela moved towards Amemne, and sat with him in front of the flickering fire. "I know…that which I seek is in that cave. But I have no way of retrieving it." Fela's eyes filled with tears. "My father is probably dead. I've been so stupid, trusting men who had other plans for me, all along. But the only thing I have left is my skill, and my father's wish, which I see now is a great wish, a powerful wish, a gift, really, he was trying to give me. And I barely heard him."

"What is this wish?" Amemne nudged her gently.

"He wanted to help me, and his friend Pib…all the people like me who are thought of as poison. This object could bring magic users…we who are called Nameless…together. It would bring hope to many." She threw a handful of pine needles into the fire. "But it's a dead dream, like my dead father. And now I am trapped here, too, like the poor man shipwrecked, like my father's friend's grandmother. Left to die."

"You won't die." Amemne smiled and rubbed her cheek with his. "You will fly away from this place one day, in the streaming golden morning, on soft winds. You will be as resplendent as the rising moon." Fela laughed joyfully at this, because it was so far fetched, and because Amemne's hands were gentle on her face.

In the morning, Fela and Amemne washed in the little beach of Seal Cove, and there Amemne told her to wait for him on the driftwood, where he had tossed in a fever just two nights ago.

She waited. Long past morning worry began to work in her, and she was about to climb the cliff again to scan the ocean when Amemne's dark seal head broke the water and he flippered ashore, humping over the rolling pebbles with his dark fin-feet, a squarish parcel clutched in his mouth. He went still, and in a kind of melting that was also a pulling away, he peeled from the winding cloak of his sealskin, his body elongating and changing and stood up from his bent knees a man, who walked on two legs. Fela witnessed this with love and awe, for she had come to love the selkie man who was Amemne. He walked to her carefully, as if getting used to his long stick-like human legs after his sojourn in the sea.

He sat close beside her on the driftwood log and placed the parcel, which was a soft gray material, on her lap.

"What is this?" She breathed.

"My dam's mother left this with our family. I... borrowed it while my people were out hunting. It is very potent, a very precious thing. It is my grandmother's sealskin, that she left us when she passed into the Great Ocean beyond. It was a great sacrifice of hers, a great gift, for it meant that she died in the form of an earth-eater." Carefully and with reverence, he unfurled the thin, soft cloak and draped it over her arm. "I thought...together, we could go into the deep cave, where your signal of magic leads, to see what might be in there."

Fela could barely breathe. "Amemne."

"The cave you seek, Afelanua, is a sacred, dangerous place to my tribe. Great evil is said to reside there. But I am cast out, and the taboos now have no hold on me." Amemne lifted his chin in defiance. "I will go with you. We will explore the place together. My grandmother's sealskin will cover you with sea magic and you can swim with me, as a seal, into the cave, to see what you will see."

Fela stroked the fine, gray fur of his grandmother's skin, and she rejoiced, but she also knew the danger. "Bullkelp."

"I know you need to go into Ana'thral. This is what we call it, the hall of demons. He may try to stop me. He may not.

I cannot let him rule me, always."

Fela shivered, though it was a bright sunlit day.

Amemne motioned for her to rise, and he came to stand behind her. He shook out his grandmother's delicate cloak of skin with great care and with equal care, he spread it over Fela's shoulders. An enveloping happened; it was gentle, as if she was being wrapped in starlight and she dissolved into a place of liquid night sky, and as quickly as she could percieve this, she was aware of the wet rocks beneath her, and Amemne next to her, and she saw humor and wonder in his dark unfathomable eye.

She followed him clumsily into the waters, and there the world became a wondrous place, filled with color and movement so that she forgot her clumsiness and let her eyes drink in the new world. Translucent cucumber green seaweeds grew in thick abundance below her, waving in the current, all in a great silent orchestration. Goose barnacles grew in a thick white carpet against the rocks as the waves crashed against them and she lost them at first, in the frothing surf, but then in the outgoing pull of the tide, she stopped, using her fins to keep herself still, as wine-red feathery fronds came out, all at once, from each little wrinkled shell and waved back and forth in the push and pull of the tide....a long legged crab on top of a rock sidled away from her, threatening with a long pincer and Amemne flitted to her side, quick as a whisper, and nudged her onward. Fela moved slowly, wanting to stare and wonder at this beautiful new world, but also knowing that they had little time. She minded the danger before them, and the task before them, and pressed on with Amemne.

He led her around the sloping rock promontory that jutted out and into the waters and, as it was high tide, he swam through the narrow cleft that led to the strange deep cavern. Before he went forward, though, he surfaced and in a great snort, took in a lungful of air. Fela did the same, wondering at her sleek new body, the fluidity all around her, and then headed into the tunnel that led into the belly of the island.

Amemne sliced forward, but here Fela balked, remembering Amemne's words about the way before them being the hall of demons. And then, remembering her father, her mother, and how she had come to this place, her heart hardened, and she tightened her will, and followed Amemne into the great gaping maw of the tunnel that led down, and down.

It was darker and colder in this close place and even here the pressures on her seal body pressed and frightened her, but she followed Amemne's form as he darted and turned through the tight tunnel that was now lightless and cold. She marveled that she could be without breath for so long.

The tunnel widened now, squatter, but longer side to side, and as she swam she became aware of a presence, like the point of a bone needle pressing on the back of her skull. Her fins, as she swam, brushed the cave wall, and cold, a cruel cold that came inside of that first wave of knowing flooded her in a jagged icy spear, and behind that came a dark, deep intent of death. A type of death that truncated thought, flattened life to a thin thread. Fela could feel her heart winding down, her breathing dying within her…every cell of her body was surrounded by the weight of the dark island above and below her and the rock of the island's body, possessed by this weight of evil, squeezed even the memory of life from her. How had she thought she could live? Dazed, her eyes closed with the thumbprint of death on them and her body sank and became still.

Her consciousness, squashed down to nothing but the

weak blue flame of her life's fire, guttered and sought desperately, in a last blind beseechment. And wildly, as her life left her, and her magic fled out from her, and images of her life dazzled by in her dying soul, the feel of a hand grasped hers hard, and in that grasp she felt the memory of muted laughter, a warm snuffling, a ribbon of pink connection. A reflected golden light of her magic came coursing back into her like a gift returned ten fold, and beneath the brutal weight of stone she felt the Ota's presence, wrapping and lightening the weight of death. Fela's fins moved. Awareness returned in a slow unraveling and she began to feel the grit of the sand beneath her pinned webbing, even with the weight of uncaring death pressing upon her. The Ota's strength shared, she pushed. It was feeble, but she pushed. She would not die here. She would not. She moved her tail and her heart quickened; she did not lose awareness of the great devouring cold but she could put up barriers against it; She held up her magic like a torch in this place of yawing emptiness and only saw more emptiness, devoid of good, staring back at her, but alongside this weight in the dark now came the presence and the sweet consciousness of the Ota, and Fela realized in a burst of understanding that the Ota's children were already being born. In the dark with the ancient immutable power of stone that ruled, she saw in a flash the desire of the rordam, to spread her children and share their strange magic, and these two powers lived together, the dark and the light. Her heart pumped and her eyes cleared. Amemne had returned to her side, circling back. She pushed away from the floor in a heave and swam true, silently thanking the Ota.

There was a straight and narrow stretch before them and she relaxed a little as warmth came back into her and as the walls of the tunnel widened, and soft white sand was below them. Amemne went up and up and the cavern's high ceiling had trapped a bubble of air! Fela breached the surface and there, on a ledge, in the dim light cast by the strange pink fungi that grew on these stones, was a gleaming black seashell. Fela could see that the strange shell had been submerged, over and over, but its form, shining, black, spiny-fingered and conch-shaped, was untouched and shone eerily in the reflected pinkish light of the submerged cave. She knew she had to get out of this place of evil as soon as she could.

Suddenly, Amemne darted off, quick as a sleek fish in a flash of movement and Fela grabbed the whelk by one of the spiny protuberances and followed him out. The heavy shell in her mouth slowed her, and she fought to keep up, as she feared one of the rival males who had hurt Ammemne was now seeking him out. Nothing good could come of this place.

The way before Fela was clear; the tunnel had no other branches to it, but she lost sight of Amemne in one of the narrow passes, and then she heard a sound that made her seal-heart falter...a great roaring shriek that screamed for blood.

Sick fear filled her and she raced forward, but she could not make the cave mouth as quickly as Amemne, and finally, as she pushed through the waters, her lungs burning and flailing with the heaviness of the conch-like shell, a scene of carnage filled her eyes. The waters around the crevice were blossoming with plumes of blood. Two seals, Amemne, and the one he called Bullkelp, were rounding on each other. Bullkelp slashed, again, and again as Amemne twisted and bit, but the older male had yellowed tusks that he dug into Amemne's flesh that the younger seal fought to avoid. Bullkelp grabbed Amemne's flipper and forced the smaller seal to the ocean floor, where he writhed. Fela dropped the shell from her mouth and raced to Amemne's side and she could see the anger, the terrible shame as she did this in his eyes, but she was beyond caring. She bit Bullkelp's tail, and as he whipped around, she sank her sharp tiny teeth into his right fin until Bullkelp roared in rage at being provoked and lashed out at her with his tail. Amemne flashed down to retrieve the shell, and Fela, who had been thrown clear as Bullkelp whipped and roared in anger, watched as Amemne took the shell and, with a speed she could only marvel at, drove several of the spiny fins into Bullkelp as he propelled himself to the older male.

The older seal thrashed silently, pinned by Ammemne for one deadly moment against the rock wall. Blood bloomed around him and the current sent slow wafting skeins of red drifting through the water. Then his thrashing grew less and less. Fela watched as the life left Bullkelp altogether and his body drifted, like a great heavy sack, off of the rock wall and toward the seafloor below.

Amemne flashed a look at Fela, still holding onto the great seashell, and together they fled and emerged on the little driftwood shore where they lay, battered and heaving, side by side, until the sun set and they slipped from their selkie skins into human ones, once more.

Fela woke. She was very cold and lay shaking on the wet tumbling rocks with seawater welling around her. Something was not right.

Amemne! She staggered up and away from the incoming tide and looked overhead. Nothing but the silvery light of the waning moons shone down, but her lover was gone. It was the deepest part of the night and she looked around frantically, but his shape, his sounds....she looked for him higher up the beach, in the driftwood, and then, as she was returning to the small strip of sand, in the water, she saw the glint of eyes in the moonlight. Dozens of dark, gleaming eyes stared at her, unblinking. She saw the seal heads turned, the moonlight glinting on the black eyes that stared, and stared.

"Amemne!" She screamed into the surf. "Amemne!" She waded into the water but her human skin recoiled from the cold. The beautiful silver selkie skin was gone. And one by one, the eyes vanished, their darker than dark lights extinguishing under the silver glow of the moons as they sank away into the impenetrable sea. All that remained to her in the silence and the vastness of the ocean was the strange seashell fetched from beneath the island, and the feel of the angry, gentle boy who knew her, and loved her well.

CHAPTER THIRTEEN

The Black Triton and an Unexpected Visitor

Fela stayed in the cove that they had shared for several days, growing thinner, pacing the beach and waiting. On this side of the island, there was less wind and the cove's seafloor was shallow and clear. At dusk, with nothing to do but ease her sore heart by staring into the glare of the water, she noticed that shoals of small fish would come into the cove, silver scales flashing as they turned in unison. So, as she waited, she went up into the meadow inland and began to cut the grasses leftover from summer and dried by winter. She fashioned mats for herself for sleeping but also mats for fishing. A lone tree hung over the cove, and she made a makeshift trap of 4 mats and a rope slung over the neck of the tree and astounded herself one evening by netting 7-8 of the small fish, easily enough for a meal. In this way, gathering food and protecting herself from the elements, Fela turned her mind from the pain of Amemne's loss.

Two weeks went by in this way. One night, she stood overlooking the ocean, her hemp sack filled with jewel clams. She had found them on a rocky prominence that yielded dozens of the large fleshy molluscs and had taken to using their empty shells as dishes. Looking out before her, Fela saw the blaze of the sun's streaming fire across the horizon.The colors of fireball-red and pumpkin orange were layered so that one bled into another like colors from the Fall leaves, her mother's paintings, sunlight through glass. Alone, her ribs jutting, her legs bandy and strong, she was as a naked whetstone in a huntsman's toolkit, alive in the moment, her heart and all of its longing resting on a thin sharp edge and waiting to be sharpened. She had the will to look on the sunset in all its glory there and exult in her life. She knew in that moment that she would return to her country, and find her father.

She walked back to her shelter with the sear of the dying sun's light burned into her mind's eye, and through every iota of flesh she felt as her own, she knew she would persevere.

She worked on perfecting her netting apparatus. She began to smoke the fish and the orange clam flesh from the jeweled shells. She wove baskets from cedar bark and one day she discovered another soul's cache. She knelt at the foot of the tree, and uncovered a longer, rustier blade than hers. Fela smiled. It would make harvesting the dried grasses so much easier. She found, also, a mouldering skeleton, part of a blanket's weave gone to the work of insects and rain, and a brooch made of a dull gold metal. She took the metal items and covered the bones as best she could.

That night after her supper, her eyes rested on the black triton. She minded the whorls on its surface, the spiny protuberances that trailed down its side like the back of a dragon's uneven dorsal ridges. Her fingers felt the inside of the mouth of the triton, smooth and satin-pink, swirling away downward into a tightly held blackness. Not thinking, wistful, desirous only to touch the smoothness with her forefinger, she reached out and felt the cool surface of the triton's inner vortex. She rested her hand there on the slide downward and closed her eyes. If only there was a way off the island. If only she could get back to her Tundin relatives and find her father. She opened her eyes and withdrew her hand. It was a moment of wishful thinking and how many times, how often had her mother told her not to dream so much? And here she was. Her own actions had gotten her here. She smiled to herself and pulled the layered grass blanket she had woven over her form, settling down in her deer moss nest to sleep.

Belador and Sauvir

Sauvir and Belador ran. Belador was not sure how he had made the strange obelisk footed with the carvings of turtles at its feet. His breath burned in his chest and his hip had gone numb and heavy from the exertion of running.

Sauvir could hardly believe the sight before them. She stood paralyzed, staring at the monster's size and the host which followed in a dark, seething cloud behind Finauld. And in that moment, clutching the flute, an image flashed before her eyes – Agadittur's general Laddahamer, leering at her, and she turned to Belador.

"Give me your sword!"

"But we have to get back...why..."

"No time." She took the sword and ran, back through the

shade-dappled path, over the old stone bridge and down into the belly of the grotto where Agadittur's naked body lay.

Gathering herself, she smote off Agadittur's head at the neck and thanked the gods she only had to strike once. She hurried back to Belador who was leaning against the obelisk, his head down, favoring the bad leg. He grimaced, smiling, and nodded to her grisly trophy. "Souvenir?"

Sauvir paused a moment to catch her breath. "I know Agadittur's men. They won't stand down without evidence of his death. This…" she held aloft the severed head, "should be mark enough his governorship is ended and proof that we did the ending."

Belador scanned the skies, his brows furrowed with worry. "Yes. Your Radthinars will need to know it. But we have the problem of the evil egg he hatched before he died, calling that monster." Belador pointed skyward. "How are we getting back home? How do we leave the Spirit City before that creature finds us?"

Sauvir smiled. "I think you hold the answer to that question in your hand."

Belador frowned. "But how?"

"You have the craft of music. Your intent may hold the key." But even as she said the words, she remembered the warning of Corva, how the flute used the player. She said nothing of her worry. The threat of Finauld was too dire. "There are hiras, the openings created by the tonkirs, in many places. I think the flute will reveal one."

Belador's eyes sought the skies and Sauvir, though she tried not to feed the fear burgeoning in her breast, did as well. The horde of dragons, their forms rippling like black swirls of ink from a pen writ in the blue skies, writhed around a central point where the more immense dragon was landing. Sauvir's heart beat high and fast in her breast. When Finauld discovered the flute gone from the pedestal....

And in that instant, a roar full of frustration reverberated even to their ears. She saw great clouds of birds flushed from the cover of trees as the monster vented his rage.

Belador took the flute with steady hands. He closed his eyes. He breathed his intent through the flute and the sound, thready at first, grew to a long, melodious tone of great though forboding beauty, a hollow sound resonant with a sorrowful timbre. He took the flute from his lips and Sauvir saw the pallor there, the great fear and also the steadfastness of his stance. "I think...there. A feeling..." He began the descent of the stairs leading away from the obelisk and into a copse of sparse trees that was below the great row of statues behind them. Sauvir caught up with him and took his waist to help his gait, and together they made the edge of the little grove. Sauvir looked behind them.

"He is coming," she whispered. And there, Belador could see, the larger creature writhing away from the hundreds of smaller dragons who rode the wind like airborne serpents, away and coming faster towards the obelisk.

"Hurry," pulled Sauvir. "It's got to be here somewhere."

"Wait." Belador closed his eyes and opened them. "Here. I know it's here...." He stumbled over a rock and she caught him, panting. "It's just ahead..."

She scented it before she saw it. It was as if the quality of air, unseen to the eye, became thinner and therefore emptier, and her hands and skin felt it before her eyes perceived it. "Belador! Here!" She looked over her shoulder. A great wind from the dragon's monstrous wings pushed and sucked through the forest and she grabbed Belador's hand and pulled him into the invisible void her flesh said was there.

Falling, lightlessness. Sauvir tried to breathe but the pressure of the place, the grip of nothingness squeezed the atmosphere from her and her eyes pressed back into her head. And then....solid ground. She fell forward onto her knees and palms and heard Belador beside her groan from the impact.

"That wasn't the same as the last time." She heard the pain in his voice and she had to laugh.

"No. But we escaped, and with the flute, and our own sorry skins." She sat for a moment in dim light, holding her head. It ached. He was right. This was not like other hira, or perhaps the passage back was more dire. She did not know. After her vision cleared, she looked around.

"Belador!" For they were back in the archives of the mages, that dimly illuminated hallway of small cubicles filled with intricate carvings. Now she could feel their individual presences, like the warmth from candles, only there was a whisper now of being, a shadow of individuality that teased at her dragon senses from each of the strange statuettes. Without thinking, without pause to worry or doubt herself, she reached for a small white spider with emerald eyes, a snakelet carved of onyx, and an owl with ivory talons.

"Are these ours to take?"

"The time for their help is now if ever there was a time. Choose what you will, but I think we must not tarry long here. I do not know if Finauld's cunning gives him the insight to find this place."

Belador's hand hovered at first over a small fish with iridescent fins, but finally he chose a bumblebee that was either carved from quartz or glass and a golden salamander, its tiny toe-like fingers delicately wrought.

Sauvir's hand sought Belador's but then she faltered.

"What is it?"

"Moon told me...but....never mind. Just follow me." Belador sensed Sauvir's anxiety, but held tightly to her hand and crossed through a dark entrance into an even darker cave.

"What is this place?" He looked around, seeing shadowy shapes like bowls on the ground, and a steady drip drip from the ceiling. There was a hollow expansiveness to the cave that made him think it opened up into an endless chasm. The feeling made his gut tighten.

Sauvir smiled at him then, a smile full of relief and love. "Moon had told me that only changelings could cross over into this point between worlds, but here you are!"

"The flute, do you think?" he breathed, putting his hand to its shape beneath his tunic.

"I don't know. Tread carefully...this place is filled with tricks that will fool your mind and your eyes."

Together they made it out of that lightless place. Night had fallen but never had Sauvir been so gladdened to have her feet on solid ground and to scent the damp soil, the blind worms' earthy work, the biting scent of pine and cedar and clean mineral odor of wet ore and rock that was their land as she knew it.

Knowing the danger of Moon's kinsmen, however, they crept back to Moon's encampment and by chance, found her solitary in her shelter, dozing by her fire.

Belador limped quietly over to the old woman's side, and placed logs onto the embers of her hearth. Moon woke, startled. "Do I see shades before me, or warm living flesh?" The old woman's face broke into a dazzling array of wrinkles as she smiled widely at both Sauvir and Belador and she sat up in her makeshift chair. "Well met, my two fawns, well met!" Then she noticed Belador's haggard look and the blood on his leggings, and the worry in Sauvir's eyes. "I see there is a story here. But let's tend that wound." She hobbled upright and moved towards herbs that hung from the rafters. She spoke over her shoulder. "What happened? Did you find the flute?"

Sauvir sighed. "We did. But there were complications."

"There always are." Moon bustled about and produced bowls, a salve and handfuls of fragrant herbs, and soon Belador's wound was being tended by both women. Belador carefully and reverently placed the flute before her.

Moon, who had fetched clean cloths, put them down and lifted the flute to her good eye. "Never did I think to see this day. But tell me. Did either of you have to call on its power?"

Her voice was so low and tense as she said this that Sauvir stopped her ministrations. She glanced at Belador, who was pale and sweating in the firelight. No one spoke for a moment.

"Yes. I did. We were on the verge of being discovered by Finauld and I asked the flute to show the way out. And...it did."

"Did anyone else use the flute? Before or after?"

Sauvir stilled. "Agadittur used it to call Finauld, I am sure of it, but...we dispatched Agadittur."

"I see." Moon sighed and very carefully handed the flute back to Belador. "Then you are now its master. You are the holder of the flute and for better or worse, your life is entwined with its life. I should have warned you, but there was so much I should have told you before you left." She closed her eyes. "What is done is done. And nothing in this world happens by chance, or so I believe." She smiled and her face lit with compassion. "Perhaps there is a reason you wield the flute. Perhaps yours is a heart full of justice and righteousness."

Belador laughed but Sauvir did not. She continued cleaning the wound. "The flute did choose well, then."

Belador sobered. He lay back down and said nothing.

Sauvir thought and her hands stilled. "What if he were to hand over the flute? To the Radthinars, or to the Palinisar of Mok Taswan? Would it be so difficult? Would the flute answer to their representatives, then, if Belador gave up his hold on it?"

"As it was told to me by my teacher, once the flute has been used by a living person, after that moment, its magic begins to entwine with the desire and intent of the one who has beseeched it. In my mind, this means that if another attempted to use the flute, time would pass before the flute gave up its allegiance to the one it had known and imprinted upon. But I could be wrong. I think we should then maintain Belador as the keeper of the flute, and where he goes, the flute should remain, until we know more."

Sauvir frowned. "Though that could come with peril, if others seek the flute for more unwise purposes."

"We have experienced this already." Belador said.

Moon raised her eyebrows at his wound. "Will you tell me what happened? Tell me all!"

They spoke deep into the night. Sauvir relayed most of their tale to Moon while Belador rested and Moon gave them counsel.

"You must return to Mok Taswan with the grisly trophy, and take back that governorship in the name of the Tundin territories, until Quint can be found, or replaced. Right now

Agadittur's appointed officers hold the city, and it's a stroke of luck you thought to bring back Agadittur's head."

"Stroke of the sword, more like it." Belador said, but his voice was low and Sauvir eyed him.

Moon laughed at the joke, but Sauvir stood. "Mother, we should rest. Belador's wounds need healing and I agree. I need to return to Mok Taswan as soon as possible, in the morning at first light." Moon stood and with a lantern, led them to the small shelter where they had originally stayed.

They built up the fire and Sauvir pulled out bedding and piled furs and all the blankets in the shelter she could find in front of the hearth. Ensconced in the covers, Sauvir turned in Belador's arms and sniffed the air. "It's the end of the second month. The two moons festival."

"Mm." said Belador, his eyes closed.

She lay back against him. "My mother used to trade for exactly 3 uzu fruits from the big market in Mok Taswan, after the worst snows had passed. We'd eat the fruit and then she would snatch the skins from me as if I was going to run into the hills with them." Belador hugged her closer.

"Mmhm." He stretched langourously. "And then?"

"She had honey put away, and she would slice the peels into strips and simmer them over night in the honey and she made this bread, Belador…with nuts, and the sweetened peel, and we would have it as a treat with cheese and wine for dinner. To celebrate the ending of winter. Sometimes we would take it to the big celebration the village had. But I loved that bread. I loved the aromatic bite of the peel, and the candied sweetness with the nutmeats."

"That's a lovely memory. Il kuru."

She turned towards him. His skin was warm against hers. "What did you call me?"

"Il kuru. Little bird, in Ennish." He kissed her nose. "My little bird." Sauvir smiled in the dark, resting in his arms. Her smile faltered. "What are we going to do? The beast is at our door. Allas is probably dead, as well as Tallisker."

"They were your friends."

"And powerful allies. And even Moon's people....half against me, half for me...their bloodlust was palpable that night."

"I remember." Belador kissed her ear. "Let's get some sleep. The daylight will bring stronger hope to our hearts. We have tools, now, Sauvir. We have each other. If you survived, don't you think there's a chance Allas Quint and Tallisker might have survived as well?"

She lay on her back, staring up at the dark rafters, envisioning Quint starving in a cage, Tallisker whipped and sold to the pirates of the Sea Realms. She tried to turn her mind from these visions. "Perhaps. But what if...what if...."

Belador reached for her gently and kissed her mouth and the silence of the evening sheltered them.

In her dreams, Sauvir flew high, high over archipelagos, islets and atolls that sat below her in the shining ocean. She knew in every fiber of her being where she was going; she had just left the mainland of Sealand's shores and was heading due northwest; she knew the names of the islands where the sea pirates roamed and had their small outlaw country in the Makkars...she knew their names, and their contours as she spied them from high above: Tuk, Pinjab, Deer, Ghost, Worhag, Skull, Spine, Witchbreath....she knew them all, as if she'd walked their shores and scented their paths, coves, briar copses, all of it. But they were not for her. She flew high and higher, into the bright searing day, with nothing but the shimmering glare of ocean below her and in the distance, far in the distance, her goal: a lone island, in between the Makkars and the mighty Sea Realms. She flew hard, for everything in her heart and soul told her to make for that island with all the power she possessed.

When she woke, the sun was streaming through the oiled window of the small shelter Moon had hidden them in. Belador had built up the fire and had brought food in bowls. Sauvir sat up and immediately began putting on her clothing.

"I have to go. We have to go. There's something I must do."

Fela was headed towards the cove on the northern side of the island where the jewel clams were plentiful. The morning was rosy and calm, and she could scent the first beginnings of spring starting; the briars' green buds were bursting forth and the birdsong was sweet around her. She was making her way down the path when she saw the four dark shapes standing, waiting for her at the cove's shore. Her blood seemed to go to her middle and her limbs grew heavy with fear. She faltered, there on the path, and for a moment, stood transfixed and still. The four shapes resolved into four women, one standing a little apart, all staring up at her with watchful, wary eyes.

Fela breathed in, and willed her feet to move. She went forward down the path to meet them.

The older woman – for now Fela could see the women more clearly – spoke directly to Fela with no preamble.

"You are the Cursed One, who brought my son to his death, the one who sleeps on this island, and sullies the very air with her foulness."

"I did not come here of my own desire." Fela whispered, still staring at the older woman. "And…Amemne…is he truly dead?"

"You should know it. You were the force behind his end."

"I don't understand." The other three women, younger, exchanged glances. Were they daughters? Followers? Fela didn't know.

The older woman stuck out her chin. "You have taken a powerful mala…a tool…from She Who Sleeps – the only way to return the balance for this is life blood, to stop the maw of She Who Sleeps from engulfing our lives. Our entire tribe would have perished had it not been for his willing sacrifice."

Fela's eyes went to the old woman's hands, which were outstretched towards her. Fela's eyes saw but her heart hung, cold and numb, a single orb of emptiness hanging in the wind blown hall of her chest.

"What is this," she whispered, but even as she asked she knew the answer.

"Before he passed he asked that his selkie skin be gifted to you. It is a taboo thing, what he asked, but he named you Ahat, wife of his heart. That is not a thing to be disrespected." She moved forward, grudgingly, and motioned to Fela to take the tawny, folded skin from her. "I have no love of you, who walk our precious land, but I am an honorable woman. I honor my son's last request."

Fela moved as if her feet belonged to a different soil, a different time. Her heart hung still, stunned into silence. Into disbelief. She took the strange smooth skin into her arms and nodded her head at Amemne's mother and her entourage. When the skin had been bestowed, all four turned with no farewell, moved for the ocean in silence, and sank before Fela into the surf, melting like the air back into the foaming brine from which they had come.

In a trance, Fela turned her back on the gold-red blaze of sunset as it broke through the circling horizon of gray sky and in the dim smoking light made her way back to her cold nest, her bag for the intended clams empty.

Sauvir flew with a lightness, a steadiness of being that made her heart ring with joy. The ocean below her sparkled and made her head ache with the brightness of it and even up here, so far above the dark-waved shining sea, constantly moving, she could scent the salt and immensity of water. And despite the weight of the fear of Finauld and what he might bring, she felt free. Free from Agadittur's binds and free from the cloying abusive touch that had lived in her mind for so long, and thankful for Belador's heart. She had lived so long by herself that she still touched that place inside of her where he lived and was surprised, each time, to find the love in his eyes steadfast. And so he lived inside of her as no one had before, and gave her great comfort, even alone as she was now and flying on a journey that was completely taken on the trust she had in her own intuition. She had left him at his family's property in the early morning several days ago, and his trust in her and her need to go made her heart soar. They had parted as two do who share each other's hearts.

She knew exactly where she was going. The sun blazed overhead, the heat of it in strong contrast to the strong cool updrafts from the ocean below. She flew and exulted in her strength and in the world around her, and knew her part in the boundless energy of nature's truth.

* * *

Several days had passed since Amemne's selkie skin had been bestowed upon her. Fela was out in the fields, harvesting the dried grasses to make more mats. It was a fine day, still cool, but the sun rose sooner and took longer to set and its warmth was strong on her arms as she gathered the grasses into a bunch and tied them loosely. She wiped the sweat from her brow and looked up. There was a shape, a dark shape flying towards her from out of the east. She stood and shaded her eyes with one hand. The shape was dark, with a wingspan that was much bigger than a bird's. The monster...had the monster Agadittur finally found her? Her hands began to shake...but the sun's light, as the shape came closer, showed gleaming black; she knew though that Agadittur's dragon skin was red, red like clay, like dried blood. This dragon, for it was a dragon....was gleaming black. She relaxed slightly and stood, the rusty sword in one hand, the gathered grasses under the other arm.

As the dragon came closer Fela stared. The huge wings beat great volumes of air and the creature's dark muscular legs came forward to touch down on the ground before her. The talons, smooth obsidian claws that came to fine dagger points, grasped the ground and the great leathery wings folded. This close to the beast, the great lungs huffed out in a hot blast and Fela covered her eyes. She clung to the sword and realized her hands had broken out into a hot sweat where metal met flesh. She kept the sword between her and the beast.

"Who...who are you?" The dragon, Fela could have sworn, turned one emerald green eye towards her and the jaw, lined with jagged teeth, seemed to smile. And then... though she watched and saw the change, the dragon, enormous, shrank, turned in on itself in a writhing convolution of flesh, scales and hair, and there before her, on hands and knees, was a woman. Fela's skin tingled with excitement and her blood coursed through her, her heart beating fast.

Pale, long-limbed and exhausted, the woman looked up at Fela, her eyes and face still smiling. "I have found you." The woman stood. She was naked, a well formed woman with short red hair and a regal stance. She began opening a bundle of clothing that had fallen from the dragon's neck.

Fela smiled too, tentatively, and her sword arm relaxed. "But...who are you?"

The woman stood, pulling on her leggings. "I am Sauvir. Ringmaker of the Tundin lands, and current sovereign of Mok Taswan, and I have come to take you home. Whoever you are. I only know that I have been summoned to take you home."

"Who told you to do such a thing?" Fela marveled.

Sauvir shrugged. "My heart. My intuition. That which cannot not be disobeyed." And Fela relaxed fully at that, for in her strange, long time on the island and all the things that had happened to her, that was the only truth she had come to believe.